Kissing Coffins
Vampire Kisses 2

"Raven is exactly the kind of girl a Goth can look up to."
—*Morbid Outlook* magazine

"Readers will love this funny novel with bite!"
—*Wow* magazine

Vampireville
Vampire Kisses 3

"A fun, fast read for vampire fans."—*School Library Journal*

Dance with a Vampire
Vampire Kisses 4

"This novel, like the first three, is never short on laughs and shudders. Alexander is as romantic as ever, and Raven is still delightfully earthy. Schreiber again concocts a lively and suspenseful story that ends on a tantalizing cliffhanger. Fans of the series will be anxious to find out whether Raven's relationship with Alexander will survive." —*VOYA*

"A good choice for Goth lovers and fans of romantic vampire stories."
—*School Library Journal*

Also by Ellen Schreiber

VAMPIRE KISSES: THE BEGINNING

VAMPIRE KISSES 4: DANCE WITH A VAMPIRE

VAMPIRE KISSES 5: THE COFFIN CLUB

VAMPIRE KISSES 6: ROYAL BLOOD

VAMPIRE KISSES: BLOOD RELATIVES

TEENAGE MERMAID

COMEDY GIRL

Ellen Schreiber

Vampire Kisses 7

—◇—

Love
Bites

KATHERINE TEGEN BOOKS
An Imprint of HarperCollins*Publishers*

To my husband, Eddie,
with love, hugs, and vampire kisses

HarperTeen is an imprint of HarperCollins Publishers.
Katherine Tegen Books is an imprint of HarperCollins Publishers.

Vampire Kisses 7: Love Bites
Copyright © 2010 by Ellen Schreiber
www.harperteen.com
Library of Congress Cataloging-in-Publication Data is available.
ISBN 978-0-06-168942-0 (trade bdg.)

10 11 12 13 14 LP/RRDB 10 9 8 7 6 5 4 3 2 1
❖
First Edition

Vampire Kisses 7

Love
Bites

CONTENTS

"I hope I find her soon, too, Raven.
I'm starved to death."
—Sebastian Camden

It was a deadly kiss—the kind of kiss that stole my breath, forced my heart into overdrive, left me hopelessly weakened and desperately gasping for more. The kind of kiss where I felt as if I'd die if it ever ended. I, Raven Madison, was in terminal bliss.

Alexander, my vampire boyfriend, and I were nestled together in the dusty depths of the Mansion's basement, passionately clinging to each other like a broken spiderweb. I'd transformed the wine cellar into a ghastly haunt as a present for him. I wanted him to have an alternative macabre sanctuary when he needed a retreat from painting in his attic room.

After Alexander's parents returned to Romania, I had decided to once again give the Mansion a feminine touch. Upon moving a portrait for storage in the basement, I stumbled across something I'd never seen before. Behind the staircase and toward the north wing of the house I found an arched wooden door secured with a heavy wooden beam. I had no idea what lay on the other side, and since Alexander was upstairs creating a masterpiece, I didn't want to disturb him. I paced in front of the door, deliberating whether to wait until he was finished. My impatience got the best of me, so I figured a quick peek wouldn't hurt anyone.

It took all my strength to pry open the beam, but less to open the rusty door. What lay on the other side was a dark, dusty, and chilly room. I was awestruck. The floor was made of uneven stones and the arched ceiling and narrow walls of gray bricks. Centuries-old Romanian and other European bottles were evenly stacked on dozens of wooden racks. On closer inspection, some of the bottles appeared different from the cabernets and merlots I'd seen resting on the three-tiered metal rack in the Madison family kitchen.

Curious, I lifted one of the Sterlings' bottles from the shelf to inspect it further when I felt an icy shadow behind me.

I gasped.

Slowly, I turned around to find Alexander standing in the doorway. I held out the bottle, which was shaking in my hand. He nodded his head, and it was then I knew—these bottles weren't filled with wine. They were filled with blood.

And now, a month later, the wine—or, rather, blood—cellar also housed votives, a portable DVD player, and an amorously entangled mortal and vampire. As the cande-labras dripped bloodred wax, my body melted around Alexander's. He, in turn, held me in the clutches of his strong, pale arms. The cool air of the cellar only added to the chills dancing up and down my spine from Alexander's tantalizing fingers. His deep, dark eyes stared boldly into mine, his fangs gently grazing my neck. For a moment, I was tempted to pull him into me—so hard he would be forced to sink his teeth into my flesh.

Then I'd be a vampire. Forever. For eternity.

But as I stared back at him, I knew that that wouldn't be fair. The quiet and reclusive Alexander had already shared so much with me—his family, his nemesis, his home. He had to be ready to take me completely into his world just as much as I was ready to *be* taken.

While I contemplated my plunge into the Underworld, three hard knocks came from above the rustic ceiling and echoed off the basement staircase walls. I wasn't about to end our embrace, but Alexander pulled away.

It was critical that nothing separate us—not time, homework, or an unwanted visitor.

I fingered his metal chain-link necklace and gently drew him back toward me. He leaned in for another kiss and I closed my eyes. As I waited for his lips to touch mine, three loud thumps echoed again. I opened my eyes to find Alexander gazing at the door instead of me.

Jameson, Alexander's butler, was out on the town catching a late-night flick with his girlfriend, Ruby White. It couldn't have been him. It was too late for deliveries, and no Dullsvillian in his or her right Ivy League–schooled mind would dare venture out to the old lonely Mansion and up its spooky driveway in the middle of the night.

"Perhaps it's a ghost," I teased. "Begging for souls."

For a few minutes, there was silence. I was relieved.

Then, suddenly, a louder bang.

"I'll only be a minute," he said, rising.

"And leave me here alone?" I argued.

"You aren't afraid, are you? I thought you felt like the Mansion was your home."

The cellar was certainly spooky, dark, and foreboding, and I was far more comforted by it than I was afraid. However, there was nothing I could do alone, and since Alexander and I were destined to be separated by the sunlight, our darkened moments together were priceless.

"Me? Afraid? Only of being apart from you."

It sounded corny, something from a greeting card or a sappy TV movie, but I meant every word.

Alexander extended his hand and led me up the basement stairs and past the candelabra flickering in the hallway.

We reached the foyer, and Alexander grabbed the door handle. I took his hand before he opened it. "Aren't you going to look out the peephole before you answer?"

Alexander glared down at me. He was, after all, a vampire. Who could be on the other end of the door that could frighten *him*?

The Mansion door slowly creaked open, and I waited anxiously to see who was brave enough to be standing in the shadows on the broken steps.

Candlelight streamed out from the Mansion, partially illuminating an unfamiliar figure. I craned my neck to get a better glimpse of the stranger. A handsome guy, appearing to be around Alexander's age, with wildly wiry short blond and brown dreadlocks, boot-shaped sideburns, goatee, and a thin, ashen face, stood before us. Tattoos crept out from his unbuttoned vintage white shirt, and gold earrings hung from his ears. He had a glistening gaze and an alluring smile.

"Dude! Where have you been?" the visitor asked enthusiastically.

"Sebastian—" Alexander was shocked. My boyfriend was familiar with the guy I thought was a stranger. "What are you doing here?"

"That's what I wanted to ask you. I had to find out from your parents that you weren't returning to Romania. But now I see why . . ." His gaze bore through me. "Well, aren't you going to introduce us?"

"This is Sebastian," Alexander said politely. "Sebastian, this is—"

"Raven." Sebastian took my hand in his. He wore more rings than I did and sported black polish on his bitten fingernails. He kissed my hand. I couldn't quite tell if this character was charming or just an annoying flirt.

"Well, aren't you going to invite me in?" he asked with a wide grin.

"Of course," Alexander replied, still surprised.

Alexander stepped back, but Sebastian didn't follow.

"Just a minute," Sebastian said. "I'll get my things."

"Things?" Alexander asked, his mouth hanging agape.

Sebastian had already taken off toward a vintage mint-condition 1960s black Mustang with silver racing stripes, which was parked in the Mansion's drive.

"Alexander . . . who is . . . ?" I began softly.

Alexander didn't answer. Instead, he remained focused on Sebastian.

The handsome visitor popped open the trunk and reached inside. I could see in the distance that he was pulling out a large duffel bag and setting it on the drive. He reached in again and placed another bag on the broken pavement. Then another.

I assumed Sebastian intended to spend the night, but judging from the amount of luggage he possessed, I wasn't sure just how many nights he planned on staying.

I wasn't sure how I felt about this stranger's visit—or move—into the Mansion. Alexander's parents left Dullsville and we were free to resume our independence. Now we were accepting boarders?

But more important, who was this person and why was he here?

"I better help him," my boyfriend said, and headed for the Mustang.

From my vantage point on the crumbling steps, I wasn't privy to their conversation. But by their gestures, I could tell the two chatted like reuniting brothers. After a few minutes, they carried Sebastian's bags back toward me. I trailed the ghostly pair back into the Mansion, up the stairs, and into one of the vacant rooms.

The room was stark and cold. A velvet eggplant-hued curtain covered a single window. There wasn't so much as a bed or air mattress. The only decoration present was a tiny vase with dead lavender flowers I'd placed on a small table a few days before.

"Appears you still like living in the past," he said to Alexander. "Where's the TV, man?"

"Down the hall," Alexander said, pointing to the far end of the house.

Alexander retrieved a candelabra sitting on a table in the hallway. He lit a match and illuminated the room.

Sebastian dumped his oversized bags on the floor. They landed with a thud, making me suspicious about the weight of his clothes. He walked around the room with the candelabra.

"Lavender?" Sebastian asked as the candles spread light on the vase.

"It's just Raven's touch," Alexander said.

"I can put it in another room if it bothers you," I offered.

Sebastian gazed down at me. His eyes glistened in the candlelight. "I wouldn't have it any other way."

Alexander stepped between us. "I'll give you some time to settle in," he said. "You must be tired from your trip."

Sebastian surveyed his new digs and stretched out his

arms while Alexander closed the door behind us.

I stopped Alexander before he moved. "Who is this guy?" I asked. "One of your relatives?"

"No. He's my best friend."

I was shocked. Alexander spoke so little about himself and Romania, I'd never heard about any friends, much less one best friend named Sebastian.

"You never mentioned you had a best friend," I told him.

"He never came up."

"Never came up? I talk about Becky all the time."

"You talk about a lot of things," he joked.

Alexander had a point. I liked to talk about every mundane thought I had during every minute of my day, while Alexander kept mum on even the most important subjects.

"So how long do you think he'll stay?" I asked. I could only wonder what it would be like for the three of us to hang out at the cemetery, my house, or the Mansion.

"Perhaps a few days."

"I thought he'd be here for weeks."

"Sebastian? He won't want to wear out his welcome."

There was one piece of information I couldn't wait to find out.

"I wanted to ask you," I whispered. "Is he like you?"

Sounds of banging and hammering came from inside Sebastian's room. Was he, too, redecorating the Mansion?

The door creaked open and I saw Sebastian kneeling on

the wooden floor, a hammer in one hand and a nail in the other. Boards peeked out of his duffel bag. It was a spookily spectacular sight—he was building a black coffin.

Alexander quickly reached for the door.

Just then we heard the locks being unlatched from the front door below.

"That'll be Jameson," Alexander said, closing the bedroom—or in this case, coffin room—door behind him. "He will have to take you home tonight."

"So soon?" I whined.

"It's really late, actually. Even Jameson's date is over."

"So what are you guys going to do? I hope you're not going clubbing."

"In this town?"

"Or hiring escorts or something."

Alexander shot me a look.

"I watch cable. I see what guys do." And these guys weren't like most others—these guys were vampires. "One of you might get hungry," I inferred.

"Don't worry. I'm the same guy with him as I am with you," he reassured.

And with that, Alexander gave me a quick good-night peck on the cheek, a stark contrast to the passionate, long lip-lock we had just shared in the cellar.

Reluctantly, I jumped into the Mercedes and Jameson drove me at a creeping pace toward my house. I caught a glimpse of myself in the rearview mirror. Reflected back was a scowl not unlike that of a four-year-old child who hadn't gotten her way.

It wasn't fair. Two guys partying at the Mansion while I had to go home to bed. If I was a vampire, I'd be able to hang out with them all night and chill out during the day near them in my coffin. I'd fit in and not have any reason to be excluded—no longer a mere mortal with a reflection and a curfew.

I fantasized that Alexander would bite me and take me into his exciting and mysterious darkened world. It had been a dream of mine to become a vampire long before I'd even met him. But now that I was dating a vampire—this particular vampire—my broad childhood desire about joining the Underworld had morphed into a specific desire—to be turned by Alexander. But so far that hadn't happened. I knew in my heart that there was the possibility that Alexander might not ever turn me, that maybe we would share life side by side but separated by our two worlds. I knew the reason he hadn't bitten me was as much out of love as it would be if he had bitten me. I'd fallen for the one vampire in the world who didn't put his needs above his morals. This only made me love him more. And I couldn't imagine that Alexander's fear might be right—that I might not like being a vampire after all, that something I'd desired all my life in its reality might not live up to my grandiose expectations. But how could that world be bad if I was sharing it with him?

And now, with the arrival of Sebastian, two immortals were partying it up in the Mansion without me.

At this point, as I was being driven home by Jameson,

I was as much disappointed about not being a vampire as I was just being me and not being included in my boyfriend and his best friend's sudden plans.

This situation would have to be fixed—sooner rather than later.

The Heart of a Vampire

T he following day, I was bursting to tell my best friend, Becky, the news of Alexander's surprise visitor. I waited impatiently by the swings in Evans Park until I finally saw her heading down the hill.

"Where have you been?" I asked, catching up to her.

"I had to drive Matt to practice. I hate saying good-bye. And yet I love saying good-bye—if you know what I mean." She giggled, still in swoon mode.

I knew what she meant and how she felt about kissing her favorite guy. But for once, I had other things on my mind.

I intently led her toward the bottom of the yellow plastic double-wide slide.

"What's so urgent?" she asked as we sat down.

"First it was Alexander's parents. Although you know I adored them. . . ."

"Yes. . . . What's up?"

"Now Alexander's best friend has invaded the Mansion."

Becky was puzzled. "I didn't know he had a best friend."

"Neither did I." I sighed.

"Wow . . . Alexander's so mysterious."

"Evasive."

"Reclusive," she added.

"Tell me about it—"

"Just like a vampire," my best friend said. "I think that's why he's the perfect match for you."

"You really think so?" I asked.

"Of course."

"A perfect match? Or a vampire?"

"A perfect match, silly. But if anyone was a vampire—Alexander could be one."

"You think so? You honestly think so?" I prodded.

"He is from Romania and has a butler. Come to think of it, I've only seen him at night," she said, and laughed. "And that garlic allergy . . ."

But I wasn't laughing.

"Did I say something wrong?" she asked.

No. In fact, you said something right, I wanted to say. Could I finally bare all the secrets to my best friend? Would she realize this time that her statements were true, instead of laughing at me when I suggested the very same thing? At last I'd be able to unleash the truth about Jagger, Luna, Alexander's parents, Onyx and Scarlet from the Coffin

Club, and, most important, my boyfriend. The load I'd been carrying in silence was too heavy on my temporarily rose-tattooed shoulders.

I weighed my thoughts. If Becky knew Alexander's true identity, then she'd surely blab the facts to Matt. I knew he was more tight-lipped than Becky. Guys didn't gossip—I didn't even know Alexander had a best friend! But this news was bigger than a footnote to a byline. This was front-page *Dullsville Gazette* breaking news. "Vampires Alive—or Undead—Atop Benson Hill." And if this information did slip out at practice or a game, then Trevor Mitchell would know. Not only would Alexander have to return to Romania, but it would be imperative that he never inhabit Dullsville again.

"What's wrong?" Becky asked.

"Alexander is a perfect match," I said with a sigh. "I was just thinking how I didn't want Sebastian to crowd us."

"That's totally normal. I get bummed when I have to share Matt with the entire soccer team. They talk about the most inane subjects, like ESPN and computer sports games. But I imagine Sebastian and Alexander are different from guys here. Is he an artist, too?"

"I don't know."

"They probably talk about world events," she imagined aloud.

"I don't even know what they talk about," I answered, clueless.

"Well, what's he like?"

"He is hot—there's no doubt about that. But other than that, I don't know. He's a total flirt and he likes electricity."

Becky laughed. "I think it's a good thing. You can find out more about Alexander through him," she said.

She had a point. Sebastian possibly held the key to the Alexander I never knew. For a moment, I lost myself in thought as I lay back on the slide. I imagined a young version of our goateed guest and Alexander having sleepovers in the cemetery, dining with Dracula's descendants, or flying in bat form over European cities.

"Is he like Alexander?" she asked, awaking me from my daydream.

"In some ways he is . . . but I'm still not sure."

"Well, we've been friends forever and we aren't the same. It should be exciting to see what he's all about."

Was Sebastian a real romantic or was he a player? Did he have a menacing streak like Jagger or more noble intentions like my own boyfriend?

"I still can't believe that for so many years Trevor and Matt were best friends," Becky said to me, breaking me out of my fantasy. "It really turns my stomach. But I'm sure Sebastian is not like Trevor."

"Let's hope not."

Becky and I were best friends but polar opposites. Were Alexander and his best friend like Matt and Trevor?

I knew one thing for sure—I couldn't wait to find out!

* * *

Unlike when Alexander's parents arrived in town, Alexander wasn't keeping me a secret from Sebastian. I was invited to the Mansion as usual. Perhaps Sebastian's arrival wasn't a bad thing after all. He could show me the side of Alexander I'd never known, as Becky suggested. I biked over to the Mansion, hoping to get there just in time for the sun to set.

I happily coasted down a hill and squeezed the brakes as I turned the corner to avoid any oncoming or parked cars. What I didn't anticipate was an obstacle of another kind—a pack of runners. I barely avoided smacking into them and veered off into a small band of hedges instead.

"Watch where you're going, Monster Girl!" I heard a male voice call.

I withdrew my bike from the bush and picked a few leaves off my hoodie.

Trevor stormed over to me, flanked by a few soccer snobs, and held the handlebars of my bike so I couldn't pass.

"Where are you off to in such a hurry?" His stunning green eyes bore through me. "A corpse convention?" Even sweaty, Trevor was gorgeous.

"What are you running away from?" I retorted. "Your mirror?"

The soccer snobs laughed. Trevor's already flushed face reddened like a sunburn.

The Mansion loomed behind Trevor up ahead on Benson Hill, the sun moments from setting.

"I suggest you turn back now. Before it's too late," he

tried to warn as only an adversary could. "When darkness falls, the monsters arise."

"The monster has already arisen," I said, in his face. "And he's standing right in front of me."

Trevor's cohorts snickered again.

"How about I just take your bike then?" He tried to wrestle the handlebars away from me, and for a moment the two of us struggled.

Finally, I released my grip. "Be my guest," I relented. "Pedal your way back to practice on a girl's bike. I'm sure it will end up on YouTube."

Trevor thought for a moment as his cohorts tried to hide their chuckles. My nemesis let my bike fall to the ground.

"We better get back. It's getting dark," one of the soccer snobs said.

Trevor locked his gaze with mine. His torment was palpable. He owned a portrait Alexander had painted of me—the only thing he could own of me. And as I stood before him, he strained with the knowledge that I was the only girl in town that he couldn't have—and perhaps the only one he truly wanted.

"Get out of here already," he finally acquiesced. "Run off to your little Monster Boy, freak."

I dusted myself off and picked up my bike. I'd have felt sorry for Trevor if he didn't bring his own torment on himself. I pushed past my nemesis and the other runners, and we both headed off in opposite directions.

I pedaled through the darkness as fast as possible. I

didn't want to miss any precious moments with Alexander and Sebastian. I felt as if I were hauling my bike up a ski hill. Exhausted, I barely had enough strength to bang on the Mansion's door. I was still out of breath and perhaps a little disheveled when Jameson let me in.

"Good evening, Miss Raven—are you all right?" Jameson stood crisp and creepy in his gray butler's uniform.

"Yes," I said. "I've never been better."

"Are you sure?" His voice and expression were kind and sincere.

I guess I appeared worse for the wear. Had there been mirrors in the Mansion, I might have been able check out my appearance. Out of respect for the Mansion's inhabitants, I didn't dare open Ruby's compact, nestled in my purse. Instead, I just combed my hair with my fingers and tried to straighten my outfit.

"I believe they are upstairs," Jameson directed.

I hurried up the creaking staircase. I passed Sebastian's new accommodations and peeked in. The once-barren room was a mess—clothes, CDs, and games were strewn all over the hardwood floor. It appeared as if he'd been living there for decades. His coffin was finished, and the lid was closed and topped with junk. The sides of the coffin were adorned with stickers of global cities—Lisbon, Beijing, Rome—like a giant suitcase.

I could hear the sounds of battle coming from down the hall.

I headed into the TV room to find Sebastian stretched out, his boots propped up on the coffee table, gaming console in one hand and a cell phone in the other. Two knights were jousting on the screen.

Alexander saw me in the doorway. He immediately rose and greeted me with concern. Sebastian didn't budge but took Alexander's absence as an opportunity and whacked his blue knight's sword against Alexander's unprotected red knight.

"Are you okay?" Alexander asked.

"Are *you* okay?" I asked. "I think he just flattened you."

"Oh, that—it's only a game."

"Do I look that awful?" I asked, suddenly self-conscious.

"You have leaves in your hair."

"I thought I got them out." I did my best to smooth out my hair.

"What happened?" Alexander asked, picking out the remaining leaves.

"I bumped into Trevor."

Alexander's sweet expression furrowed. "In the woods? Did he hurt you? I'll—"

"No—I just hit a bush. I should have hit him instead," I teased.

Alexander shook his head. I knew he was tormented, just like Trevor, but for different reasons. Alexander felt the need to protect me from all evil—vampire and mortal. He was tortured, knowing that during the daylight hours it wasn't possible for him to safeguard me against my nemesis.

"I'll pick you up from now on," he firmly instructed.

When my parents put me under curfew, I rebelled. However, when Alexander was overprotective, it made my heart race.

"Trevor—who's Trevor?" Sebastian finally said, pausing the game and typing on his cell phone.

Though the Mansion was as decayed as an ancient ruin, I was disappointed with Sebastian's lack of refinement. Instead of behaving like a guest, he was sitting like he was in a fraternity house, scuffing the already antique coffee table with his shoes. I wasn't Miss Manners myself, and heaven knows I wouldn't have cared if Becky had put her John Deere, soil-stained boots on my bed. But this was the Mansion, after all, the house of my dreams, and, more important, Alexander's home. I spotted a beat-up old ottoman in the corner and scooted it in front of him.

"You might be more comfortable," I said graciously.

"Thanks," he said. "Now I feel like a king. I can see why you like it here," he said to Alexander.

I didn't know if he was sincere or making a snide remark.

Alexander sat on the couch, and I curled up next to him.

I was curious about this friend who seemed like the opposite of Alexander.

"So how do you like it here so far?" I asked.

"Awesome, now that I've found a room with outlets. And I can't believe Alexander still doesn't have a cell phone. How do you two communicate—by smoke signals?"

"Excuse me?" I asked defensively.

"It's okay—he's just joking," Alexander reassured me.

"Oh . . . ," I said, relieved. My first response was to protect Alexander. I hadn't been exposed to anyone before who amiably ribbed my boyfriend.

"So who are you texting? A girlfriend?" I wondered aloud.

"One of many," Alexander said. "A lady in every town."

"It must be nice to receive steamy texts," I hinted to Alexander. "I'd cherish every one."

Alexander only shook his head.

"Oh . . . yeah," Sebastian said. "I'm being rude, aren't I?" After a few clicks, he closed his phone.

Sebastian sat up, now ready for conversation. "So, what did you do all day?" he asked. "Soak up the sun?"

"Hardly. I was stuck in school. How about you?"

"Well, my day started about two minutes ago."

"Yes, that's what I figured. So . . . it's really cool you came to town. I haven't met any of Alexander's friends."

"He likes to keep us hidden—like tucked away in a vault somewhere."

"So do you live in Romania, too?" I inquired.

"Yes. We lived next door to each other."

I imagined two Gothic mansions resting on top of a large mountain surrounded by fog, witchlike trees, and a ghostly cemetery and protected by a full moon.

"I guess you didn't live in the suburbs?" I asked.

"Not exactly."

"Do you live in a mansion, too?"

"I guess. I never thought about it really. It was just our home. But we had lights," he said, giving Alexander a verbal jab.

"Do you know Jagger and Luna?"

"Vaguely. I wasn't there for that whole covenant thing. I crossed paths with Jagger, but Luna was a mortal . . . so I never saw her. My family travels a lot."

"Are they art dealers like Alexander's?"

"No—they are pilots."

"Are they all—"

But before I could say vampires, Alexander placed his hand on mine. "So many questions. Don't you want to save a few?" he hinted politely.

"Finally, a woman who is interested in me for a change," Sebastian said coyly. "And a beautiful one, at that." He flashed a mesmerizing smile. "So what do you want to know?"

Sebastian was charming, no doubt about it. But my interest was in Alexander. I wanted to know more about Sebastian but even more about my own handsome boyfriend.

"Are you homeschooled like Alexander?"

"Yes. But we took night classes together. We had to take a few for exams. Alexander helped me pass them—without knowing it."

"So what was Alexander like?"

"I think it's time we figure out what we're going to do," Alexander interjected.

Sebastian ignored his host. "Ah . . . that's the real question. About Alexander. You were working your way through me to get to him, weren't you?" he asked. "It's okay. I'm used to it. Alexander always got the girls," he revealed.

"Oh, really?" I asked. I couldn't bear to imagine Alexander with any other girl than me. I felt a sword of jealousy pierce straight through my heart.

"Something about long hair and being an artist," Sebastian added.

I bit my black lip. Alexander shot Sebastian a cold stare.

"Maybe we should go," I said.

"Don't worry," Sebastian said sweetly. "He broke many hearts. That's why I had to check out the girl who made him stay. Most keep him running."

I felt relieved and flattered at the same time.

"So what about you?" I asked. "Where is your girlfriend?"

"Me?" he asked. "I don't have one."

"I figured with all your travels . . . ," I said.

"True love has always eluded me," he confessed. He spoke in a charming and intimate tone, as if he was baring his heart for the first time.

"So, what are you looking for?" I asked.

"Someone kind, sincere, and captivating. Someone unlike anyone else I've ever met."

"Someone like Raven?" Alexander said proudly, giving me a gentle squeeze.

"Yes, just like Raven." Sebastian grinned. "But without the artistic boyfriend."

"Then I'm sure you will find her," I reassured him.

Sebastian gazed at me with a stare so bold, yet sincere, that tiny hairs rose on the back of my neck. "I haven't found her yet. But I'm hoping my true love is closer than I think."

"Well, I hope you find her soon," I said.

Alexander switched off the game and TV. "Let's get something to eat."

We all rose and collected our things. As Alexander returned the remote to the TV stand, Sebastian leaned toward me so closely his goatee brushed softly against my cheek. "I hope I find her soon, too, Raven." He whispered in my ear with such intensity that chills raced down my spine. "I'm starved to death."

3 A Trip Through Dullsville

I wasn't sure what Sebastian's opinion of Dullsville would be. It certainly wasn't London, Paris, or Lisbon. He, like Alexander, had been to places I'd seen only in Armstrong Travel's brochures.

As we sauntered down Main Street, past the courthouse, fine restaurants, and trendy boutiques, I held my crimson-streaked head high, knowing that I was in the company of two vampires and that glaring Dullsvillians weren't aware of their true identity.

I had to admit we were a motley crew. Sebastian sported his wild dreadlocks, shining rings, and snake tattoos. Alexander was gorgeous in his studded leather jeans and white T-shirt, while I danced around the sidewalk in a dark knit hat, torn black-and-red minidress, and midcalf lace-up boots.

Townspeople, decked out in their designer jeans and

Kate Spade bags, avoided us as if we were the stars of a freak show. But I loved it! I felt triumphant being surrounded by what I thought was normal. Though Dullsvillians gawked at us, I sensed that most of them were staring at me, wondering who I thought I was, drawing such negative attention.

"That's it," I said when we reached the Main Square's fountain. "That is our bustling metropolis."

"This town is really quaint," Sebastian remarked.

"Yes, different from what you are used to, I suppose. Instead of the Eiffel Tower, we have a ten-foot-tall bubbling fountain. And instead of the Roman Colosseum, we have Dullsville High's stadium."

"No, I like it. I can see why Alexander and his grandmother moved here."

"You do?" I asked. "Did you know Alexander's grandmother?"

"I never met her. She moved here years ago and rarely came back to Romania to visit. But I hear she was a wonderful woman."

"I hear that, too." I squeezed Alexander's hand tightly.

"So . . . ," Sebastian continued as we passed Shirley's bakery, "where does one go in this town for a bite?"

"I can treat you to some ice cream," I offered. "Shirley's has the best in town."

"That's not what I was referring to . . . ," Sebastian said.

"Then what exactly were you referring to?" I pressed. It wasn't every day a girl from Dullsville got to hang out with two sexy vampires.

"Where are the babes in town?" he said, licking his fangs. "I mean besides you, of course."

I wasn't sure if Sebastian was serious about finding a meal in the form of a girl. Even though he was Alexander's best friend and surely benign, he was a true-blooded vampire.

"Probably at home studying or shopping at the mall," I finally said.

"No bars?" he asked.

"None that you'd like or that we could get into."

"So where do you two go for fun?"

"The cemetery," I answered.

"There are girls there?" he asked, surprised.

"Not living ones," Alexander said.

We all laughed.

"Yeah, I guess not," Sebastian said.

"I figured you'd love cemeteries," I said. "Alexander does."

"Sebastian would rather hang in an Internet café," Alexander told me.

It was not the atmosphere I'd imagined Alexander's best friend—much less a vampire—preferring. But perhaps I rushed to judge him, as so many of the students at Dullsville High judged me.

"Well, there's one right there," I said, pointing across the street to Javalicious.

Sebastian perked up. "Let's grab some coffee."

"All right," Alexander said.

Great, I thought. Here I was hanging out with two

hotties from the Underworld, and we were going to sit in a mundane coffee shop?

"And we'll sip it by the tombstones," Sebastian suggested as if reading my mind.

Happy and giddy, I linked arms with Alexander, and the three of us headed for the shop.

I tried to pay for two jumbo-size caramel mochas with whipped cream and one hot chocolate, but Alexander insisted on treating us. He beamed like I hadn't seen before, basking in the company of his two best friends.

An elderly couple sharing a pot of tea seemed preoccupied by our presence.

"Dude, did you see her checking me out?" Sebastian teased as Alexander dropped a few dollars in the tip jar.

The woman rose and made her way toward us.

"I think she heard you," my boyfriend said, taking his hot chocolate.

"I do like older women," Sebastian whispered, "but this one is using a walker."

The woman slowly approached Alexander, who towered over her. The demure lady had two circles of soft blush on her powder-white skin. Alexander politely stepped aside, assuming she was going to order.

She was quick to grab his hand. "Are you the Sterling who lives in the Mansion on Benson Hill?" she asked.

The two baristas ceased brewing and the entire shop of coffee klatches eagerly listened.

Alexander looked as if he wasn't sure how to respond. No one in town had ever talked to him before. Even though the elderly woman wasn't threatening, we were still uncertain of her motives.

"Uh . . . yes," he finally replied.

"We have a Sterling painting hanging in our home. I bought it at the art auction last month. We were told it was by an up-and-coming Romanian artist. Is the artist a relative of yours?"

"Yes, a very distant one—" Sebastian interjected before Alexander had a chance to speak.

I was surprised by Sebastian's remark, especially since it wasn't true.

"Are you kidding?" I asked. Alexander was too humble to speak up. "Alexander's the artist," I announced proudly.

My boyfriend glared at me and shook his head.

"But you are so young," the woman complimented. "It couldn't be you."

"It is!" I said, glowing. "Isn't he wonderful?"

"My husband would love to meet you . . . ," she said, referring to the older gentleman seated at her table. "If you have a moment . . ."

"Uh . . . I appreciate that—" Alexander began politely.

"Perhaps another time," Sebastian interjected again. "We really should be going."

Like a savvy media handler, Sebastian whisked us away from the woman before she could ask any more probing questions.

"See, I told you Alexander attracts the ladies," Sebastian lamented. "If only she were sixty years younger."

Sebastian was leaning against an already tilting tombstone while Alexander and I were nestled together on a cold cement bench.

"This town is relaxing," Sebastian commented, gazing at the stars. "Besides that curious woman, no one really bothers you. You could hide out here forever and no one would notice."

"I think they notice," I corrected. "And most of the people do bother me."

"Not when I'm around," Alexander said.

"True. I'm lucky; I have a bodyguard." I took a sip of coffee. "Speaking of bodyguards . . . Why didn't you guys talk to that couple? I figured you'd want to tell everyone about your paintings."

"It's probably best not to . . . ," my boyfriend said.

"You don't have to be humble," I told him. "But I must confess it is an endearing quality."

I rested my head on Alexander's shoulder, and he gently stroked my hair.

"In this case, it's survival," Sebastian said. "Would you like Alexander to be run out of town?"

"Of course not," I said, sitting up.

"Then he can't become the next Picasso," he added.

"But he sold his paintings to half the town," I challenged. "They are bound to wonder who painted them."

"Yes, and then they'll be asking questions. Who is this mysterious artist that lives on Benson Hill? Why does he live by candlelight? Why does he sleep in a coffin?"

"I wasn't planning on telling them what he is, just who he is—an amazing artist," I defended. "You know that, Alexander."

"Of course," he reassured me. "I don't think we have to worry. She was just a kind and elderly woman. I don't think she'll be asking for a tour of the Mansion anytime soon."

"You're right," Sebastian conceded. "Far be it from me to come to town and upset what you've established here. You have a really sweet setup. But for me . . . I need more. . . ."

"Excitement?" I wondered aloud.

"No."

"Wi-Fi?"

Sebastian leaned toward us and glanced around. "Vampires," he whispered.

I was surprised by his candor.

"I'm not sure if I could be the only one in town," he admitted to me. "That's why I always admired Alexander. He seems comforted by the things that frighten me the most."

I melted at his compliment for my boyfriend. I'd always regarded Alexander with such high esteem, and I blushed knowing that others did as well. Alexander must have been touched, too, because a warm smile came over his face.

"This is a great place for someone like us," Sebastian said, stretching out again. "If you don't mind being the only immortal."

Sebastian's remark filled me with loneliness for my

boyfriend. Maybe Alexander was better off not being the only vampire in town.

"Do you think you'll move here, too?" I asked. "Then Alexander wouldn't be the only one."

"Actually, I'll be taking off in a few days," Sebastian replied. Alexander didn't seem surprised, but I was disappointed.

"But you just got here," I said.

"I never stay in one place too long when I travel. . . . Don't want dust to collect on my casket."

"But we're having so much fun. Aren't we, Alexander?"

"Yes—" But Alexander didn't need to respond. His face showed a contentment I wasn't sure Sebastian had ever seen.

"Besides, I'm cramping your space," Sebastian said.

"It's a mansion," I said. "All it has is space."

"Yes—you can stay as long as you like," Alexander said. "You know that."

Sebastian surveyed Alexander and me hand in hand, cuddling on the bench. Then he gazed off into the distance. "Perhaps I need to add a bigger city to my collection. And, who knows, I might get lucky and meet someone there like you did here."

Sebastian took a swig of his coffee, crushed the cup in his hand, and tossed it into a garbage can. He popped in his earbuds and began dancing his way around the tombstones.

"Looking for someone you know?" I asked.

"You never know who you'll find at one of these places."

Where Alexander had found a moment of peace, Sebastian was restless. He was searching for himself in the many cities plastered on his coffin. But just like in Barcelona, New York, Rome, and the many other places he visited, he hadn't found a home in Dullsville.

Not only was I caffeinated—I was confused. It was more than a giant-size caramel mocha that was creating my insomnia. I lay awake in bed, clutching Nightmare as she fell asleep in my arms. How could she sleep so peacefully when so much was going on? At first I didn't want another visitor in the Mansion, but now, after meeting Alexander's best friend, I wasn't ready for him to leave Dullsville. Sure, he was disorganized and messy, but he had an insight into Alexander that I couldn't get without him.

And I found myself feeling a little jealous that he had the freedom to fly off to the bright lights of the cities far away. I could only imagine what it would be like to have the opportunity to monster-watch at Loch Ness, search for witches in Salem, or camp beneath Dracula's castle in Romania.

Also, I was getting a little attached to Sebastian. It wasn't only that he was more playful than the other vampires I'd met, like Jagger or Luna, but I was concerned how Alexander would feel when his friend left him behind. I couldn't imagine a happy existence without Becky by my side.

First Alexander's parents left, and now his best friend would be going. Could this mean that Alexander would want to leave, too? Their visits and eventual returning to his homeland, Romania, might remind him of what he'd been missing since his own arrival in Dullsville. He had roots with his vampire family and friends. And if he didn't turn me into a vampire, would he eventually become lonely surrounded by mere mortals? I began to wonder if I could possibly be enough reason for him to stay.

Alexander appeared confident and content in the company of our cryptic clique as we entered Hatsy's Diner. He hummed "Love Me Tender" as Elvis's voice crooned throughout the fifties-themed restaurant.

Once again our odd threesome was met with glaring eyeballs, but my immortal companions appeared unaware. Sebastian seemed immediately taken with the charm and authenticity of the diner and was intrigued by the jukeboxes. While the vampires picked out a few songs, I found Becky sitting in a red vinyl booth, texting.

I plopped down across from her. "Where's Matt?" I asked.

"He has to study. But he says hello." She held her phone in front of my face. It displayed the words *L8TR QT* followed by *Tel R Hi*.

I waved to the phone.

Although I loved that Alexander was reclusive and shrouded himself in mystery, I did wonder what it would be like if Alexander had a phone and I could receive sweet nothings on my phone—*LUV U LOTZ, Can't W8 2 C U, A X R.* I had a million girlie texts from Becky and quite a few nagging ones from my mom but nothing close to the love notes Becky was receiving from Matt.

Suddenly, Alexander and Sebastian were standing at our booth. Alexander's black hair hung sexily over his deep, dark eyes, his white collar perched up around his neck, and he wore a dark jacket and tight jeans. His Underworldly cohort, Sebastian, stood with his hands in his oversized pockets, sporting sparkling earrings and wildly woolly locks.

"Becky," I began. "This is Sebastian."

Sebastian and Becky locked eyes. They both froze for a moment that lingered like an extra heartbeat. There seemed to be an electric charge that surged between the two. His pale face flushed ruby red. She giggled without a sound.

"Come sit down," I said, hoping to sever their strange and sudden connection.

"Oh yeah," Sebastian said, as if coming out of a fog. Becky quickly shut her phone.

Alexander scooted next to me and placed one hand on my red-and-black-striped tighted knee and the other around my shoulder. He smelled yummy in his lightly scented Drakkar, and my pulse quickened.

Sebastian inched awkwardly onto the bench next to Becky. The seemingly self-assured guy appeared suddenly shy and smitten. He tucked his hair behind his ear and played with the rings on his fingers.

Becky held her purse tightly in her lap like a child's teddy bear and nervously twisted the nylon strap.

"I hope you're hungry," I said, and handed Sebastian a menu that sat behind the tabletop jukebox.

"You know I am," he mumbled.

Sebastian fidgeted in the booth and tapped his fingers against the menu. Becky avoided him by flipping through the jukebox songs.

Dixie, a familiar waitress, came over. She wore her hair in a black beehive, and her curvy figure was squeezed into her white uniform like a forties pinup girl's. When she wasn't reading a tabloid magazine at the soda counter, she was heckling her customers. She had a heart of gold but little patience for the teen clientele.

"What'll you have?" she asked.

Sebastian hadn't had time to open his menu; he was too busy perusing Becky. "What are you getting?" he asked Alexander.

"The malts are fabulous," Alexander said.

"Order anything you'd like, Sebastian," I said.

"Anything? Or anyone?" Sebastian gave a cheeky wink to my best friend.

Sebastian waited for her response. Embarrassed, Becky blushed and giggled. Sebastian took that as a positive sign and he, too, grinned.

Alexander chuckled and I sneered. I was the only one not finding any humor in his comment.

"Four chocolate malts, four burgers, and two atomic fries," I said to Dixie.

"Sounds good to me," Becky said.

"How do you want the burgers cooked?" Dixie cracked her gum so loud it sounded like a car backfiring.

"Rare," Sebastian said.

Alexander kicked Sebastian underneath the table.

"Rare?" Becky asked.

"We don't serve hamburgers rare here." With the tip of her pen she pointed to a small disclaimer on the bottom of the menu. "This isn't a five-star restaurant, if you hadn't noticed. You can order your burgers 'burnt' or 'not burnt.'"

"Then four not-burnt burgers," Alexander said with a grin.

Dixie blew a pink bubble, winked at Alexander, and wiggled toward the kitchen.

We all cracked up, and when our laughter subsided there was an awkward silence.

Sebastian checked out Becky, which caused her to fiddle with her napkin.

"Alexander and Sebastian grew up together in Romania," I told her. "Just like us, best buds."

"That's great," Becky said demurely. She wrung the napkin again.

Since no one else was talking and I was dying to find out more about Alexander, I figured this was as good a chance as any to steer the conversation in that direction.

"So what did you two guys do for fun in Romania?" I asked.

Alexander shrugged his shoulders. "I don't know—we just hung out."

"And played golf?" I asked.

"No." Alexander laughed. "We did the things kids do—"

"Yes—but you weren't normal kids."

Becky appeared puzzled.

"I mean, since Alexander's grandmother was a baroness," I said, covering my comments.

Dixie returned with our shakes. Becky hid behind hers and the rest of us began to devour ours.

"Did you get into trouble?" I asked.

"I did—" Sebastian said. "But Alexander was always there to get me out of it."

I nestled into my boyfriend.

"What do you do for fun?" Sebastian asked Becky.

"Me?" she asked, surprised the conversation was directed toward her.

"Yes."

Becky leered at me as if I were going to answer for her.

Sebastian waited, but Becky didn't answer. She just played with her straw.

"We do girlie things," I answered for her. "Talk, gossip, and talk some more."

"Do you like cemeteries?" he asked.

"Me?" She shook her head vehemently.

"Was Alexander in his attic room painting like he is now?" I asked.

"Uh . . . yes. He always was working on some masterpiece. But he rarely showed me. He kept them hidden in an armoire in his room. Do you paint or draw?" he asked Becky.

"No—I'm not an artist."

"Did you guys go clubbing?" I asked Sebastian.

"Sure, sometimes. Do you like to go out, Becky?"

"Uh . . . me?"

"Alexander," I said, clearing my throat. "I left something in the car. Can we go get it?"

"Uh . . . sure," my boyfriend replied.

Sebastian reached into his back pocket and handed Alexander his keys.

Once Alexander and I were outside Hatsy's, I stopped.

"The car is over there," Alexander said.

"I didn't forget anything. I wanted to talk to you."

Alexander was perplexed. "What do you want to talk about?"

"What is going on with Sebastian?"

"What do you mean?"

"I'm trying to have a conversation with him and all he wants to do is talk to Becky."

"He doesn't mean anything by it. He's just being polite."

"Does he think we were fixing him up?" I asked.

"I don't think so."

"Well, he needs to back off. Don't you see the way he's staring at her? He's hitting on her."

"I think you might be overthinking it," Alexander said soothingly.

"Did he ask me one question?" I charged.

Alexander paused. "Is that what this is about? That he's not paying attention to you?" he asked sweetly. "He doesn't always have the best manners. I do try to tell him. . . ."

"No—I don't care that he doesn't ask me."

But perhaps it did bother me. Maybe I was getting wrapped up in his attention toward Becky. Maybe I was oversensitive to his advances since they were not directed toward me. I felt like a heel, accusing Alexander's friend of preying on Becky.

"Okay, okay. I guess I'm just being overprotective of Becky, like you are of me."

When we returned, Sebastian was holding Becky's hand and reading her palm. "This is your life line—and this is your love line." He was seductively tracing her lines with his finger. "Very strong indeed."

"See?" I whispered to Alexander.

"Now I'll show you mine." He scooted closer to her and held out his palm.

Becky giggled uncontrollably. She glanced at a long line running through his hand. She had a quizzical look on her face. "Wow—your life line seems to go on forever."

Now Alexander wasn't pleased with Sebastian's flirting.

"How about you tell them about the time you drove your Mustang through the cemetery and it almost fell into an empty grave," Alexander prompted his friend, taking charge of the situation.

Just then Dixie arrived with a tray full of food. Sebastian tore into his burger while Becky picked at her fries.

I could tell she wanted to say something to Sebastian. Normally, Becky was painfully shy, but with Sebastian's playful attitude toward her, she was loosening up. "What do you and Alexander do all day while we go to school?" she asked suddenly.

Sebastian was pleased with her interest. "Sleep."

"You sleep all day? I can't imagine not getting up when the sun rises."

"Well, I stay up all night."

"Like Raven? She has insomnia. She'd sleep all day and go to school at night if she could."

"Or not go to school at all," I chimed in.

They laughed, but I was serious.

"You are so different from other girls I meet," Sebastian said.

Becky slunk down. "I know—I've never been to Europe or even New York."

"No—I mean that as a compliment," he continued.

Becky lit up. She wasn't used to being paid so much attention by a good-looking stranger.

"Yes, Becky's the greatest," I praised. "Not like those other girls in school who are obsessed with everything Gucci. We've been friends since the third grade."

"I can see why you like it so much here," Sebastian said to Alexander. "The people are really genuine. And cute."

Becky turned as red as the bottle of ketchup she was reaching for. She squeezed it over her fries but then left them untouched.

"So, Alexander," I said, taking over. "Now we know what we do all day. What do you do?"

Alexander sat up as we waited for his response.

"I spend it thinking about you, of course."

After stuffing our faces with burgers and chocolate malts, Alexander gallantly paid Dixie and we headed for the parking lot.

We escorted Becky to her truck underneath a star-filled night sky.

"It was great meeting you, Sebastian." She opened her arms to give him a friendly hug. Alexander cleared his throat when Sebastian squeezed her a bit too long.

"When will I have the pleasure of seeing you again?" Sebastian asked. Clearly, Sebastian didn't want our visit to end.

Becky twisted her hair and shrugged her shoulders. She gave me a quick hug, hopped into her truck, and rolled down the window.

"Good night, Raven," she said. "I'll talk to you tomorrow. Good night, Alexander."

We watched and waved as Becky drove out of the parking lot and down the street.

"So now what do you want to do?" I asked. "Hang out at the cemetery again?"

"I guess we should be dropping you off," Alexander said.

"Me? But the night is so young," I moaned.

Alexander put his arm around me and we headed for the Mustang, but Sebastian continued to stare in the direction Becky had just driven.

"What's up?" Alexander asked him, tripping him out of his trance.

Sebastian was silent.

"Hello. . . . Are you in there?" Alexander prompted again. "Is something wrong?"

"I don't know," Sebastian said. "I've never felt like this before."

"Are you sick?" I wondered.

"I think . . . I'm in love," Sebastian announced, as if it was just occurring to him.

"With who?" I asked. "Dixie?"

"I can see why you like it here, dude," he said to Alexander. "You found your soul mate, and now I've found mine."

"Who are you talking about?" Alexander asked.

"Becky."

I laughed. But then I could see that Sebastian was dead serious.

"She has a boyfriend," I said.

"She does?"

"Yes," I said emphatically.

"Of course she does. Someone as pretty as her. But does that matter—in the long run?" Sebastian mused.

"It matters. Besides, she's not really your type."

"AB negative? I like all kinds." Sebastian didn't seem

to be joking, but Alexander broke a smile.

"It's not funny," I said. "I think it's time to go—"

"I'm not laughing," Sebastian said. "It aches in here," he said, pointing to his heart.

"That's not love, that's indigestion," I said. "Hatsy's is known for it."

"I can't shake it."

"We can stop at the pharmacy and get you some Rolaids," I offered.

Sebastian faced me intently. "This isn't heartburn. Don't you see?"

"All right," Alexander said, putting his hands on Sebastian's shoulders. "It's time we head out."

"Did you see how into me she was?" Sebastian asked. "Asking me all sorts of questions?"

"She was just being polite," I told him.

"I like that. Most girls I meet are into themselves. Can you give me her number?"

"Her number?" I asked, alarmed. "But she already has a boyfriend!"

"Something I can overlook. For now."

"I really don't think . . ."

"One cannot dodge Cupid's arrow," Sebastian proclaimed.

I rolled my eyes. "Cupid isn't the only one with an arrow." I scowled.

Alexander rubbed my neck. "It's okay. He's just playing."

We got into the Mustang, and as Sebastian drove me home, the ghostly duo boisterously sang to tunes blasted from his speakers. I pretended to not be disturbed by Sebastian's off-key singing or his sudden proclamation.

Sebastian waited in the car while Alexander escorted me up the front steps.

"Why didn't you say anything about Becky?" I asked when we reached the door.

"He's harmless. He falls for girls all the time and whines when they don't fall back. I was surprised he didn't declare his love for you." Alexander fingered my belt loops and drew me to him.

"Yeah, why didn't he?" I asked, gazing up at him.

"I'm sure he did," he said, brushing my hair away from my face. "He just knows what I'd do to him if he did anything about it."

"You think he'd really like me?"

For a moment, I too was as giddy as Becky had been. Not because I liked Sebastian but because I liked the idea of being admired. I spent so much of my life in Dullsville being ostracized, it was exhilarating to know that I might be attractive to the male species, especially when the male species was the vampire kind.

"How could he miss the most beautiful girl in Dullsville—or the world, for that matter?" Alexander asked. "He'd have to be blinder than a bat."

My boyfriend stared at me, his chocolate eyes burning through me. He leaned into me and gave me a five-star kiss.

The following morning, I was lumbering around my room in a towel and Jack Skellington slippers like a lost zombie, vacuously trying to figure out what to wear to school, when I heard Becky repeatedly blast her truck's horn. I threw on the first thing I saw, a charcoal-colored T-shirt dress, and layered it with a ripped Wicked Wiccas tank, gathered my backpack, and haphazardly dragged myself out of my house. When I got into her truck, Becky was sporting an overblown grin.

"What's up?" I asked.

"He texted me like a hundred times." She blurted out the words as if she'd been holding them in for a decade.

"Who?" I asked. But I already knew the answer. "Sebastian?"

She tried to hide the smile that crept across her face by chewing on her sparkling pink lip and drove us toward school. "How did you know?"

"A hundred?" I asked flatly.

"Well . . . not exactly. But I'm going to have to buy more minutes."

"What did he say?"

"He wanted to know what I was doing . . . what I liked to do . . . what were my favorite flowers." Becky beamed.

"Did you answer?"

"I did until Matt texted in. Then I told him I had to go."

"You shouldn't be texting Sebastian."

"Why?"

"Why? Because you have a boyfriend."

"I know that. But it's no big deal."

"Are you kidding?" Becky was as serious as she was naive. She was so amazed that Matt liked her, she couldn't fathom that another guy might possibly feel the same. "Texting another guy? In some countries you could be jailed."

"Raven, I think you're totally overreacting."

"Me? Overreact? Promise me you won't text him anymore."

"He was just being nice."

"He's not being nice. He's dangerous," I blurted out.

"He's a criminal?" Becky squealed.

"Of course not," I said, and sighed.

Becky was being unusually stubborn. I knew it was because she simply didn't think I wasn't going to leave her in the dark anymore. I had to use all my ammunition.

"He's dangerous for different reasons than you think. He's in love with you!"

* * *

The sky over Dullsville was picture perfect—beautifully blue and dotted with bright, puffy clouds. It didn't match the storm I felt brewing inside me during lunch as Matt questioned Becky and me about Sebastian on the bleachers.

"I have to meet this dude," Matt said, wiping his mouth with the back of his hand. "He's either a real gentleman or a real snake. Giving flowers to another guy's girl? If he did that to my girlfriend, I'd have to take him out."

Matt had grown up as Trevor's shadow. Now that he'd broken away from Trevor's clutches and started dating Becky, he showed a confidence I didn't know existed. That said, he still was far from the type of guy to throw the first punch—or the last, for that matter.

"Why don't we talk about something else?" I suggested. I was trying to eat organic peanut butter and jelly on a million-grain roll my mother had bought at some overpriced health food store. Becky fingered her gluten- and flour-friendly roast beef sandwich. She noticed my distaste and happily traded lunches with me.

"Does Alexander know Sebastian gave you flowers?" Matt asked skeptically.

"No, he doesn't," I said.

"Are you going to tell him?"

"Uh . . . I guess."

"I think it's important to be honest in a relationship," Matt said. "Becky and I always tell each other everything. No secrets."

Becky hid her face in her hands. "Matt, there's

Becky almost slammed on the brakes. "You're joking."

"No—it's true."

"No one's ever been in love with me. Not even Matt."

"What? Of course Matt loves you."

"Well, he's never said it."

I was surprised. I figured Matt told her all the time, as Alexander told me.

"Are you sure?"

"Yes, I'm sure. I would have told you the minute he told me."

"I just assumed he already had. But clearly, he doesn't need to. It's written all over his face."

"You think so?" she asked with doughy eyes. "You know how I feel about him."

"Of course he loves you. That's why you have to stay away from Sebastian. So you don't spoil your relationship with Matt."

"I'd never let that happen. But I don't believe you about Sebastian. Truly, he was being totally innocent."

"Guys don't want to be just friends. Haven't you seen *When Harry Met Sally*?"

"No."

"Well, perhaps it's time you watched it."

"I'll rent it tonight."

"Perfect. Then we're done with the subject," I ordered. "He's supposed to be leaving soon anyway, so there's no need to mention his name."

"Mention whose name?" she asked with a cute grin.

Becky parked the truck in the student parking lot. We

dashed up the front stairs through the bustling hallways and hurried to our lockers. She opened hers to find a glass vase tied with a white ribbon and filled with tiny pink roses.

"Wow—Matt never gave me roses before," she exclaimed. "Didn't I tell you I had the best boyfriend ever?"

My stomach tied itself in a bigger knot than was on her bow.

"My guess is they aren't from him," I mumbled.

"What?"

"Uh . . . nothing. Is there a card?"

"Oh . . ." She picked through the flowers. "Here it is. 'Until we meet again . . . Sebastian,'" she read aloud. "Sebastian?" My best friend was as shocked as she was flattered. She stuck the card back in the vase.

Suddenly Matt appeared behind us. Becky gasped and turned corpse white.

"Did you miss me last night?" he asked with a churlish wink.

"I did," I said truthfully.

"Thanks, Raven."

Becky tried to envelop the flowers in her unbuttoned paisley cardigan, but her sweater was too small and a few buds peeked out from her neckline.

"Where did you get those?" Matt asked. "You don't have a secret admirer, do you?"

Becky froze. She never lied to Matt—or anyone, for that matter.

"They are mine actually," I fibbed for her. "She w holding them while I shut my locker." I held out my har

Becky opened her sweater and I took the vase.

The bell rang and Mrs. Hathaway, our history teach opened the door for class.

"I didn't think pink was your color," Matt s bewildered.

"Uh . . . It's not. I'm regifting."

"I can't believe you'd give away flowers from Alex der," he charged.

"They aren't from him—" I said, trying to defend actions. Then I realized what I'd said.

Matt spotted the card poking out of the vase. snatched it before I could stop him.

"Sebastian?" he read. "Alexander's friend? Why i giving you flowers?"

My horror story was spinning out of control. I w even sure what I was saying anymore.

"Uh . . . we're going to be late for class," I said.

"Yes," Becky agreed. She took Matt's hand and led into class before our story got any more fictional.

I handed Mrs. Hathaway the bouquet. She was surprised and a little skeptical of my gift but happily pl the vase on her desk.

Becky and I glared at the bouquet. Even under no circumstances I couldn't focus too long on history. N with Sebastian's roses prominently displayed in class, Becky and I were distracted. For once, neither of us lea a thing.

something you should know—"

"Did I tell you Sebastian won't be in town much longer?" I suddenly asked. "He's just passing through. So surely we can talk about something else."

Becky paused. "Yes," she agreed. "Let's talk about—"

"That's a shame," Matt said. "I would like to meet Alexander's best friend. I imagine he's pretty cool. What's he into?"

He's into Becky, I wanted to say.

"Gaming," Becky said. "He looks like a modern-day pirate," she said, half dreaming. "All he is missing is an eye patch and a pegleg."

"Maybe I should be the one worried about him honing in on my girlfriend."

Matt gave her a bear hug as she blushed.

"How about the five of us hang out tomorrow?" he continued. "The team is going to Hooligans and you guys can come, too."

Hooligans was a grown-up version of Chuck E. Cheese—without the oversized rat. I'd gone there on a few occasions when Billy was still being called Nerd Boy. My little brother loved the video games and I loved a night out.

I wasn't sure if Hooligans was going to be Alexander and Sebastian's idea of fun, but I was more concerned with Becky being in the magnetic vampire's presence again.

"I'd rather spend time with just us," Becky said. "I haven't seen you—"

"Yeah—the guys have been keeping late nights," I said truthfully. "They might want a night off. And more important, who wants to see Trevor?"

"It's a big place. You won't even run into him," Matt said encouragingly. "Besides, if Sebastian is leaving, when will you get a chance to see him again?" Matt asked, excited by his idea.

"I was hoping not anytime soon," Becky whispered to me.

"Awesome," Matt declared. "We'll meet this week. But I'm warning you, Raven, if you open your locker this afternoon and find a ring, then I'm telling Alexander."

As soon as the sun set, I hopped on my bike and motored toward the Mansion. It was imperative I get to Alexander posthaste, and this time I wasn't going to let anyone stand in my way—not even a handsome soccer snob. I was fortunate that all I had to dodge were a few cars and a woman walking her poodle.

I pounded on the door until Jameson politely let me in. I paced on the squeaky parlor floorboards for what seemed like an hour until Alexander finally entered the room.

Alexander was dreamy, standing in the doorway, his long black hair tousled and slightly damp from his shower.

"You have to talk to him . . . ," I exclaimed. "I have to talk to him."

"What? Talk to who?" he asked.

"Sebastian," I said, racing over to him.

I was so harried, the note card fell out of my hoodie pocket and onto the floor. Alexander picked it up before I could place my boot over it.

"'Until we meet again . . . Sebastian'?" he read aloud.

Alexander's dark eyes turned angry red. "What is my best friend doing giving you cards?" he asked, his brow furrowing.

"It wasn't a card, Alexander. It was flowers."

Alexander looked shocked, then angry. He couldn't hide a feeling of betrayal as his expression tightened. "Sebastian!" he began to call.

I grasped his arm. "They weren't for me."

"Then who were they for?" he asked skeptically.

"Becky. He texted her all night and then had roses waiting for her in her locker."

Alexander was only partially relieved. Now he was confused. "Why would he do that?" he asked softly.

"You heard him last night. He said he loved her. . . ."

"I know, but I didn't think he meant it. Besides, he's copying my moves. Leaving surprises in your locker— well, Becky's."

"He has to stop, Alexander. Becky isn't used to this kind of attention. And he is, after all . . ."

"Like me?" he asked with a hint of sadness.

"No one is like you," I said, taking his hand.

"Sebastian has never acted like this before. . . ."

"To make matters worse . . . Matt wants to meet him. He has no idea the flowers were for her. He thinks they were for me."

"Who gave him that idea?" he asked, slightly accusatory.

"Well—"

"So now everyone at school thinks my best friend is hitting on my girlfriend?"

"First of all, he's not. And second, no one knows."

"You're sure?"

"Of course. How would they, anyway? No one talks to me—just about me."

He glanced away. I knew it was painful for Alexander to imagine me at school without him. "I just wish—"

"Just say the word and I'll quit," I said, wide-eyed.

Before Alexander could remind me of the importance of my education, I pulled him close. "Matt wants the five of us to go to Hooligans."

Jameson shuffled into the room with a tray of two bloodred smoothies, each garnished with a tiny blue plastic sword and three cherries. Alexander took one and I picked up the other.

Jameson's bulging eyes bulged out even more. "Miss Raven, that is for—"

"I'll save you the trip."

I marched up the staircase, followed by Alexander, careful not to spill the bloody concoction, and pressed my ear to Sebastian's bedroom door. I could hear the sounds of footsteps on the squeaky floors, followed by a thud.

"Room service," I called.

The door creaked open. Sebastian's hair was sticking up like a starburst. He was sitting on his closed coffin in boxers, a black wrinkled shirt, and unlaced boots and was staring at the cell phone in his hand. Socks, T-shirts, and bandannas were scattered around his coffin like the dirt from his homeland.

"What happened to you?" Alexander asked.

"I didn't sleep. I've been up all day."

"Well, here's your breakfast," I offered, almost shoving the drink at him.

"I'm not thirsty."

"Oh, yes you are. I need you well nourished."

He examined the smoothie and fiddled with the tiny sword.

"Try it, you'll like it," I encouraged him.

He made a face. "Anybody, is there a vein in the house?" he called.

Alexander laughed.

"It was never fun dining with the Sterlings," Sebastian continued. "When the Camdens had people over for dinner—we really had them for dinner," he joked like a vaudevillian comic.

"Drink up," I demanded.

I watched Sebastian as the red liquid slowly made its way up the straw, past his full lips, and into his mouth.

I thought he'd be repulsed, as one would be tasting sour milk. But he appeared to enjoy it just as any mortal might a strawberry shake.

"Raven tells me you sent flowers to Becky at school?" Alexander asked.

"I didn't send them," he emphasized.

"Whatever—however," Alexander said. "The point is . . ."

"I know. . . . It's just . . . I've never felt this way. Really.

I see how you two are. I feel that way about Becky."

"May I remind you that Becky has a boyfriend?" I said firmly.

"What would you have done if you thought Raven had a boyfriend?" Sebastian challenged Alexander.

Alexander had experienced that kind of situation when he saw me with Trevor outside the Mansion last Halloween. My boyfriend thought carefully before he spoke. "It's not the point what I'd do. . . ."

"See?" Sebastian said. "I can't forget her. Besides, people break up all the time."

"Becky and Matt will never break up." I hadn't imagined that scenario before, and I shuddered at the thought. "She's going to get married to him."

"Married? She's still in high school."

"When she gets out. And she certainly isn't going to date a vampire!"

They both looked at me. I had just stuck my combat-booted foot in my black-lipsticked mouth.

"I mean that in a good way," I said. "I'm the one who likes vampires," I declared. "But Becky has a thing for mortals."

"I'm sorry, Raven, I can't change my feelings," Sebastian said sincerely. "What am I supposed to do?" he asked with an almost childlike quality.

"You can change what you do about them," Alexander said. "Raven's right. You have to back off."

Sebastian cooled down. "I know. I just couldn't sleep all day . . . waiting and wondering when I could see her again."

"Well, you'll get to see her tomorrow night," Alexander revealed.

"Really?"

"Matt wants the five of us to hang out," Alexander said.

"Who's Matt?"

"Becky's boyfriend," I stressed

Sebastian turned toward the window. The moonlight cast a glow against his sad and almost lonely expression.

Perhaps once he saw how happy Becky was with Matt he'd be cured of his feelings for her.

Sebastian snapped back with a wicked grin. "Great! I'll be on my best behavior."

6

Becky and the Barn

The students at Dullsville High treated me more oddly than usual the next day when I arrived at school. Apart from the usual shifty glances thrown my way, I heard more whispers and mutterings than normal. I was throwing my coffee in the trash when I felt a person standing behind me.

"Your secret admirer is not so secret anymore," a male voice said.

I tried to ignore the demon in khakis and inch around the trash can, but he blocked my escape. Cornered, I spun around.

Trevor towered over me. His golden locks were combed perfectly, as if he'd just been primped for a photo shoot. I didn't have the energy for one of his trivial confrontations.

"Do you mind? Littering is illegal, you know. Be my

guest and do us all a favor," I said, gesturing toward the can. "Throw yourself in."

"I love it when you talk dirty," he said, not budging. He placed his hand against the wall, blocking my exit.

"I really don't have time for you today," I said, and slipped underneath his human barricade.

"Two-timing your boyfriend takes a lot of time and energy, does it?"

This time I stopped and faced him squarely. "What are you talking about?"

"Word has it there's a new monster in town and he's leaving gifts in your locker—candy, jewelry, love notes."

I was always amazed at how fast rumors spread throughout Dullsville and how grossly incorrect they could become.

"No one is leaving me anything."

"Is that so? Then what were those flowers doing on Mrs. Hathaway's desk?"

"Teacher Appreciation Day."

"That's not until . . ."

"I was planning ahead."

"I'm not going to even react to your lies. I thought when you ditched your boyfriend, the least you could do was come to me. After all, I'm much better-looking."

"I didn't ditch Alexander!"

"Then he doesn't know?" he asked as if he was unraveling a mystery. "You are two-timing him."

"You've wasted enough of my time. . . ."

"Or are you having a monster threesome up there in

that filthy mansion? You always seemed the kinky type with your studs and boots." He sidled up to me, so close I could feel his warm breath against my neck.

"No—you have it all wrong." I faced him hard. This was one time I'd rather have been in class than out in the hallway. "I have to go. . . ."

"Well, someone is going to know about you sneaking around—and it might be Alexander." Trevor thumped me on the head and disappeared into the crowd of students.

I wasn't dating Sebastian. There was nothing to hide from Alexander—but by the way everyone was treating me, the whole school must have believed I was cheating on him. My boyfriend, like any other, would not have been happy about that.

After school, I was at Becky's waiting for sundown. The time had slipped by as Becky typed away at her computer doing research for an English paper and I ignored my own homework by lying on her bed, rereading *The Vampire Lestat*.

"I think I'm almost finished," she said gleefully.

"Well, I should be going," I said. The sun was slowly sinking; only a few rays still poked out behind the field. "I need to tell Alexander that the whole town thinks I'm dating Sebastian before it gets back to him."

"I'm sorry things have gotten so far out of hand. If you hadn't stuck up for me . . ."

"That's my job," I said. "I'm your best friend." I hopped off her bed and grabbed my jacket. "I better get my bike."

When we arrived at her house, Becky and I picked apples from one of her trees for a snack, and I'd parked my bike in the barn.

Becky peered out her window. "Why don't I drive you home instead?" she asked with concern. "It's totally dark out there."

"That's okay. I can find my way."

"But there aren't lights," she said. "Even in the barn."

I'd always protected Becky—at school, in town, in life—but this was her property and she wasn't normally afraid on her own land.

"Don't worry," I reassured her as I walked down her creaky stairs. "I can go by myself. It will just take a minute."

"The light switch hasn't been working, and quite frankly it's kind of spooky without it," she confessed.

"I'm all about spooky!"

"I'll drive you home," she insisted.

"You don't have to do that. Besides, I love wandering around fields in the dark. Maybe we'll find a dead body."

"Don't say that!"

Once outside, Becky picked up a flashlight from on her back-porch railing. "I never get used to coming out here in the dark," she said.

It was pitch-black except for the tiny light beaming from her flashlight. We had at least fifty yards to walk just to reach the barn. The cool night air made the journey even more chilling.

Becky dug her nails into my arm but was doing her best to be brave.

I thought I'd take her mind off her fears as we traipsed down her gravel road and through the darkness. "So are you sure Sebastian hasn't tried to contact you again?"

"No."

"No texts? Or flowers?" I hinted.

"Nothing," Becky vowed.

"You'd tell me—"

"Of course I would. You know I can't keep secrets."

"Good." Perhaps Alexander's and my talk was getting through to him. "If you weren't going out with Matt— would you like him?"

"But I am going out with Matt."

"If you weren't," I prodded.

"But I am, Raven."

"You haven't even thought about it?"

"No—why would I?"

As we grew close, a neighbor's horse whinnied in the distance.

The old barn smelled like hay and old wood.

For a moment, Becky struggled, but she opened the barn door. "It sticks," she said.

The barn was dark as a cave. Becky shined the light inside. Tools hung from the walls like dripping wax.

"What happened to the switch?" I asked.

"It shorted out the other day. My dad didn't have a chance to fix it."

We were blind except for the thin beam from her flashlight. Something felt strange—like we were being watched. I knew that there weren't any farm animals kept in the barn.

I wasn't sure what else it could be.

"Hurry and get your bike," she said.

Becky was still hiding behind me, pointing past the tractor. She clung to me so hard, I couldn't move.

Just then we heard a rustling in the rafters.

Becky jumped. "Ooh! It's a bat. My dad said he saw one the other night. I figured you'd want us to catch it for you, but it was too high."

"It's more than a bat," I surmised.

After a few moments, the bat disappeared. I sensed someone lurking in the shadows. I took the flashlight and shined it on a bale of hay. Nothing. I shined it again on a workbench. Becky hid behind me, grasping my shirt so tight I could barely breathe.

"I'm scared, Raven. Let's go back."

I shined it on the tractor. The light caught the tail edge of blond dreadlocks.

"Sebastian?" Becky said, shocked.

I turned the light away from the vampire. He approached us in the moonlight, pushing my bike.

"What are you doing here?" I asked. "You're supposed to be with Alexander!"

"He was painting and I wanted to get some air."

"In Becky's barn?" I charged.

"I was walking around and I heard some girls talking. I had to investigate." He smiled broadly.

Becky seemed to buy his excuse, but I knew better.

"You scared us to death—well, at least me," she said. "I'm so glad it's just you."

"I'm sorry," he said. "Truly. I'd never want to make your heart race. Unless it was for a good reason."

Flirting time was over. "You're lucky Becky's father didn't find you. He has a shotgun," I warned.

"He rarely uses it," Becky said. "You must be tired if you walked all the way from the Mansion. Can we get you a drink?"

"No—" I answered for him.

"Sure!" he said over me.

I took my bike from Sebastian and the three of us headed back to Becky's house. In Sebastian's presence, she was no longer afraid and didn't cling to me in any way.

Becky offered us fresh lemonade. Becky had the best lemonade I'd ever tasted; her mother made it from scratch. Both Sebastian and I gulped it down and asked for seconds.

"It's time we go," I said.

Sebastian wasn't ready to go. He wandered around her kitchen, examining every picture and decoration.

Where was Alexander when I needed him? If he had a cell phone, I could text him immediately. Instead, I tried to ring the Mansion's line. If Alexander was painting, his music was probably blaring. It was true. The phone rang endlessly.

Even Jameson didn't pick up.

"No voice mail—really frustrating," Sebastian said.

"Aren't you in town to visit Alexander?" I asked.

"Well, yes."

"Then why aren't you two hanging out?"

"We don't spend every minute together. We're guys."

When Becky and I got together, we spent every minute in each other's company. But guys? Sometimes when Henry was over with Billy, one would be on the computer while the other was playing video games. I often wondered why they got together in the first place.

Still, I wasn't crazy about Sebastian's behavior. It didn't seem to be bothering Alexander, however, if he was creative enough to paint. And for all I knew, Alexander might have needed the space.

"We better be going," I finally said to Sebastian.

"I can drive you both back if you'd like," Becky offered.

"You can drop Raven off first, then me," he said.

"Becky will drop us both off at the Mansion," I instructed. "Then we can tell Alexander where we've been."

After Becky drove us to the Mansion and I placed my bike against the gate, I grasped Sebastian by his sleeve and pulled him toward the front door like a scolded child.

"See you tomorrow at Hooligans," Sebastian called back to Becky.

We met Alexander in his room as he was washing out a brush in a small bucket.

"Did Sebastian let you in?" Alexander asked.

"Well, yes, but . . ."

"Did you go into town?" he asked Sebastian. "It did me good to get some work done."

"Yes, I had a great time seeing the sights," his best friend answered.

Alexander was euphoric from painting. I hated to spoil his mood by telling him where I'd found Sebastian.

"I'm really such a lucky guy," Alexander said. "My best friend and girlfriend are here and I'm almost finished with my new project." He pointed to a covered painting resting on the easel. "But this one is for me."

Sebastian clearly wasn't going to tell Alexander what he'd been up to. I strongly suspected that if Alexander found out Sebastian had been lurking in Becky's barn, he might throw Sebastian out of the Mansion. I didn't want to snitch on him, but I wasn't about to keep secrets from Alexander.

I had a major dilemma on my hands.

I gazed at Alexander, who was relishing his creation and his friends. Alexander was so peaceful, I couldn't bear to tell him Sebastian was stalking Becky or that Trevor was saying I was two-timing him. But then Sebastian surprised me.

"I happened upon Becky today when she and Raven were together," Sebastian confessed.

"Happened upon?" Alexander inquired.

"Alexander—I'm hooked. I just wanted to see her one more time."

"He flew into her barn when Becky and I were getting my bike," I said lightly. "Nothing serious."

"You can't be sneaking around her house," Alexander reprimanded. "That's immature. And dangerous."

Sebastian frowned.

I was the queen of sneaking in places. I wasn't any better than him.

"No more. I've washed my hands of love." Sebastian seemed to sense that this was upsetting his best friend. "We'll stay in for the rest of my stay and play Medieval Mayhem. I won't see her anymore. Not now, not ever."

"But we are supposed to see her and Matt tomorrow at Hooligans," I said.

"Well, I suppose one more time won't hurt, will it?" Alexander said.

Sebastian's face lit up. "I'll have on my game face."

7

Videos and Vampires

The following afternoon, Becky, Matt, and I were hanging out on Dullsville High's soccer field waiting for practice to begin. Sebastian's fascination for Becky indelibly stuck in my mind. Matt and Becky were nestled together by the home-side goal—not even the threat of an opponent's score could break them apart. As my best friend gazed up at her beau adoringly, I realized I'd never imagined Becky with anyone but Matt. He was the first boyfriend she ever had and I never doubted that someday they'd be married, live a quiet life in Dullsville with a couple kids, and have the proverbial white picket fence. Even a handsome and love-struck vampire so far hadn't turned her head away from her one true love.

Sebastian had fallen for a girl who could make him happy—if only she liked him back. I was hoping that that would never happen. Not only didn't I want Becky to become a vampire, but I didn't want her to be with anyone besides Matt. But I felt empathy for Sebastian. He didn't choose his amorous fate.

As the two lovebirds snuggled, I sat alone thinking about my own relationship with my boyfriend. We had bigger challenges that faced us on a daily basis besides an immortal paramour. It was as simple as the sun and as complicated as immortality.

Alexander was my soul mate. But was our love strong enough to face the inherent struggles of our two different worlds? If he didn't turn me, would that ultimately come between us? Could we live mortally together while he lived eternally alone?

As I watched Becky and Matt cuddle, I felt my love for Alexander was not a choice. It was otherworldly.

Alexander's life would surely be easier if he were dating a vampire. He wouldn't be in a position to make a life-altering decision. Perhaps I was putting too much pressure on him for my own needs. He didn't want to turn Luna, so why would he want to turn me?

And would my life be any easier if I were with some-one mortal? We could see each other by our lockers, share classes, and hang out at school dances. But I lived in Dullsville, where no mortal was like me. Even if Alexander hadn't moved into the Mansion on Benson Hill many months ago, I would never have found anyone here to love. I viewed my lonely, mortal world before I met Alexander as far more difficult than the challenges I faced by falling in love with a vampire. The insecurity of Alexander's and my future was better than the certainty of my unhappiness without Alexander.

Hooligans was a noisy, technology-driven themed restaurant. The food was normal fare—salads, chicken wings, sandwiches—but the selling point was the jumbo-size, high-decibel, flashing-light video, pinball, and dancing games. Some games spit out tickets to use like cash to purchase prizes like bears, bracelets, and pencil toppers. It was quite easy to spend a hundred dollars just trying to win a twenty-cent prize.

Alexander thrived in his quiet hideaways, like the Mansion, Dullsville's cemetery, and the Coffin Club, under the guise of Phoenix. I was concerned that Hooligans was going to blast him into sensory overload. However, I knew Sebastian would be in gaming heaven.

Sebastian parked his Mustang in an empty space right next to Becky's truck. He wore a spectacularly stylish bloodred blazer. Alexander glowed—his hair rich-looking, seductively dangling down, his lean body pressed into black jeans and a white T-shirt and finished with a sparkling oversized skull belt buckle.

We arrived at the hostess stand to find a long line and at least a dozen patrons with pagers.

"We'll be here all night," Sebastian said.

"Follow me." I forged through the sea of people and pushed myself right in front of the main hostess.

"We're meeting two friends. I'm sure they already have a table," I said in my most mature voice, as my parents did when we were meeting their friends for dinner.

"You can go ahead and check."

We squeezed our way through the waiting customers—screaming babies, young couples, and corporate parties. I was counting my blessings. So far no Trevor or a soccer snob in sight. I found Becky and Matt at a round table in the corner of the restaurant.

Before any formal introductions could be made, Matt extended his hand to Alexander's best friend. "Hey—you must be Sebastian."

But Sebastian's focus was instead on Becky, and Alexander nudged his best friend.

"Oh, yeah. Nice to meet you."

Sebastian made his way to the empty seat across from Becky, but I snuck in behind him and scooted myself into the chair just as he landed on my lap.

We looked quite the sight—as if a ventriloquist had just sat on the dummy.

"Hey—get off of my girlfriend," Alexander teased, jabbing Sebastian.

We all laughed as Sebastian rose to find that the only empty chair was between Matt and Alexander.

Matt and Sebastian found a common ground talking about computer games. However, in between breaths, Sebastian continued to be fixated on Becky, as if he was trying to seduce her with his gaze. Any normal guy could be a pest, but a vampire? He could be deadly.

I held my menu out, blocking his line of sight, until the waiter finished taking our orders and the menus.

"We can all use my points," Matt offered, showing us his Hooligans game card. "Let's go."

The gaming area was packed—filled with couples dancing, skiing, shooting, and bowling.

Matt took Becky's hand, Becky took mine, and I took Alexander's. Matt led us through the maze of people while Sebastian followed close behind.

Matt stopped in front of the only unoccupied game—a pinball machine, Nosferatu's Nightmare.

"Want to play?" he asked, challenging Sebastian.

"Sure," Sebastian replied. "Winner gets the girl."

"What girl?"

Sebastian gestured to Becky, who turned bone white.

"You're joking!" Matt said.

"Of course I am." But I knew Sebastian really didn't want to be. He appeared lovelorn for my best friend.

However, Matt and Sebastian played like they were competing for more than a high score on a pinball machine.

I cozied up to Alexander. "Are you having fun?"

"Absolutely!"

"Wouldn't it be cool if Sebastian didn't leave?" I asked. I was happy that Alexander had companionship—someone his own age—in the Mansion.

"It would be awesome. Maybe we can convince him to stay a bit longer."

Nosferatu's Nightmare was a ghoulish 3-D game. Silver balls shot through winding tubes with neon bats running across them, and squeaky coffin lids opened and closed in attempts to catch the ball.

"Open Dracula's coffin—one thousand points," a monsteresque voice commanded as Sebastian hit the ball over a gravestone.

Becky rested her head against Matt. Sebastian couldn't concentrate and lost the silver ball. He relinquished the controls to Matt and stood next to Becky.

Matt pulled on the lever and clicked the flippers. A graphic of fangs clenched down on a woman's neck flashed on the video screen along with the sound of a woman screaming.

"It's not really like that," Sebastian said to Becky.

Matt was just as naive as Becky. He, like she, was missing all the obvious signs that another guy had fallen for his girlfriend. And, most important, that the other guy was a vampire.

Matt scored a massive number of points and kept the ball in play like a professional gamer. Even Alexander was engrossed. Matt politely gave the controls to him. "Here—try it."

The four of us watched as Alexander clicked the flippers as if he'd been doing it his whole life. The ball hammered the bumpers, skyrocketing his score. He got multiball after multiball and racked up points in the millions.

We all cheered as "Highest Bloody Scorer" came across the screen and the machine lit up with blinking red and white lights.

"Alexander seems to be in heaven," Becky said as we moved to another game. "I think it's great that his best friend is in town. I know it's been good for Matt, too. Since he and Trevor stopped being friends, he does seem a bit lonely. Now he has two new ones."

Two Jet Ski simulators opened just as we approached them.

"Let's do this!" I exclaimed.

Becky and I each hopped on a machine. Matt gestured to Sebastian for him to ride along with Becky as Alexander sat behind me.

Sebastian was tentative as he settled on the ski behind Becky.

"Put your arms around my waist," she said, lacing his hands around her. "You don't want to fall off."

Matt swiped the card before Sebastian could change his mind.

Suddenly we were off, jetting over waves and avoiding wayward motorboats. I could almost feel the heat from the Miami sun, the ride felt so authentic. I peered back at Sebastian, who was hanging on to Becky for his life.

"Slow down!" he said as if we were really tearing down choppy waters. "Slow down!"

Becky let go of her throttle as I passed her and a half dozen computer-generated opponents until we soared through the finish line.

Alexander and I hopped off our Jet Ski, while Sebastian still clung to Becky.

"It's over," she said. But Sebastian didn't move.

"Want to do it again?" Becky asked.

"I don't think so."

"Need some help?" Matt asked.

Instead of being thrilled by the ride and embracing his crush, Sebastian was green. Matt handed him a soda he had just bought. "Here, drink this."

For the next several hours the five of us danced, boxed, and jousted our way through Hooligans.

Alexander and the gang hung back at the table while Becky and I counted and cashed in our skeeball earnings tickets. Becky and I each had enough tickets to win a stuffed bear—Becky pointed to a sparkling teal blue one, and I spotted a shimmering black bear.

The girl handed the blue bear to Becky. Just as the cashier was about to take the black one, another worker grabbed it.

I sneered. "Hey, that was my bear!"

"I'm sure it's going to a nice kid, though," Becky said, trying to ease my disappointment.

Just then, we saw it was Trevor holding the black bear.

"Kid, yes—nice, no," I remarked.

"That was our last one," the girl said. "They weren't very popular, so we stopped ordering them. We have tons of pink ones."

"I ought to rip it out of his hand," I told Becky.

Alexander, Sebastian, and Matt were mesmerized watching two men battle it out on Lazer Wars. I didn't want to bother Alexander with my swiped winnings.

"Haggling over children's toys, are we?" Trevor said, sidling up to me. "So is that Alexander's competition? I guess he hasn't heard of a brush before."

"I didn't want this one," the Pradabee whimpered to Trevor, tugging on his Polo. "I told you I wanted a pink one."

The Pradabee's voice was like black fingernails on a chalkboard—and not in a good way.

Trevor glared at me and flung the black bear on the counter as his date retrieved a new plush.

I grabbed the bear, which had landed on its back, and dusted it off.

"You're lucky you're going home with Raven," Becky said to the bear. "The alternative would have been disaster."

Matt and Alexander were settling the bill while Becky, Sebastian, and I headed outside. Sebastian engaged Becky in conversation. He fawned over her in a genuine love-struck manner, complimenting her hair and comparing her beauty to that of a famous actress. She was so mesmerized by his attention, she didn't see a small row of bushes in front of her and tripped and fell onto the sidewalk.

Sebastian and I immediately rushed to her side.

"I'm okay," she said with an embarrassed laugh.

"Are you sure?" I asked, picking up her bear and handing it to her. "Who put that bush there, anyway?" I joked.

Becky wiped off a few leaves and raised up her skirt just above her knee to expose a small wound. There was blood.

I shielded her knee and gazed up at Sebastian. He stood, frozen as if now he was the one in a trance.

"It's nothing," Becky said. Then she noticed Sebastian's odd behavior. "It's just a scratch. I hope you aren't the kind to faint around blood."

"I don't think he's going to faint," I said, watching Sebastian.

"Do you have a Band-Aid?" she asked me.

I wasn't sure what was in my Corpse Bride bag. I kept my gaze on Sebastian at the same time feeling my way through my purse—I recognized a pen, lip gloss, mascara, and loose change. Finally, I pulled out a piece of paper. "We can cover it with this." It was an old detention slip.

"That's not sterile. Do you mind checking with the hostess inside?"

Sebastian was still fixated on Becky's wound.

"I'm not leaving you here." I tried to block her from Sebastian's sight line. "We need a tourniquet. Immediately." I took off my Olivia Outcast hoodie and attempted to tie it around her knee.

"Raven—it's hardly even a cut!"

Before I knew it, Sebastian was crouched down next to Becky. He took her leg and placed her sandaled foot on his knee. Her pink toes sparkled against his black pants like tiny stars. It was like Prince Charming trying to fit the glass slipper—only this Prince Charming was a vampire.

Becky giggled awkwardly, her leg in Sebastian's grasp.

"I'm all right," Becky said. "It's just a scratch."

Sebastian examined her wound as a jeweler would a diamond ring.

"Why are you two making such a fuss?" Becky asked.

Before I could do anything, Sebastian took his index finger and wiped her wound.

"Oooh . . . that's gross!" Becky screeched, closing her eyes.

Droplets hung on his finger like red wine.

His fangs flashed. He reached his finger to his mouth.

I knew what he was about to do next, and though I wanted to see it for myself—a firsthand account of a vampire following his instincts—I knew if Becky saw it we could never undo the damage that would incur.

His finger was about to pass his lips.

"No—!" I exclaimed.

I pushed Sebastian as hard as I could away from Becky, and the two of us tumbled to the ground.

"Raven—what are you doing?" Becky asked.

Sebastian and I lay on the grass, for a moment disoriented. I regained my bearings and rose to my feet to find Sebastian already standing. His pale face was cherry red. I grabbed his hand and held it toward the light. The blood on his finger was gone.

He gazed at me with childish horror, like a toddler who has broken into a candy jar.

Becky took out a crumbled tissue from her pocket and dabbed it on her wound. Then she showed me. "See? The blood is gone."

Alexander and Matt suddenly were standing behind us.

"What's going on?" Matt asked, concerned.

I shot Alexander a stern glare.

"Nothing really. I tripped and skinned my knee,"

Becky said. "Sebastian was very brave and wiped the blood off with his fingers."

Matt led Becky into her truck while Alexander's contentment slowly turned to anger.

Alexander's best friend was leaning against his car. A wicked grin overcame him as he licked his pale blue lips.

As Sebastian drove toward my house, I tried to mask the severity of the situation by chatting about the upcoming weather forecast. I didn't want to snitch on Sebastian—to condone or deny what had just taken place—if only not to spoil Alexander's evening. My boyfriend had been so happy to be out of the Mansion with his best friend by his side—a fellow vampire, a childhood playmate, his next-door neighbor. A guy with whom Alexander could be his true self—no longer having to wear the disguise of a rebellious mortal but instead that of a sensitive vampire. But Alexander was keen to Sebastian's ill conduct. The two friends rode in silence.

When we finally parked in front of my house, Sebastian, along with Alexander and I, got out of the car.

Alexander didn't bother to shut his door. He avoided Sebastian altogether and started for my driveway.

Sebastian tapped his boot against his tire in disgust.

"He didn't mean to do it," I defended.

Alexander chewed on his lip.

"Alexander—" Sebastian said bravely, confronting his best friend. "I don't know what happened. I'm truly—"

Alexander faced his friend. "You crossed the line," he

said in a tone that couldn't hide his disappointment.

"I didn't plan on it. It wasn't like I hurt her. I couldn't help myself; I'm not restrained—like you," he said sincerely.

"You can't stay here," Alexander said firmly. His voice was strong, but it couldn't mask how it pained him to say it.

"I'm sorry, Alexander. I won't go near her again."

"Becky didn't see anything," I said. I wasn't sure why I was defending Sebastian. Perhaps it was because the hapless vampire, like me, seemed to get in trouble just by breathing.

"Tomorrow night," Alexander started, "when you wake up, Jameson will have your things packed."

Sebastian slunk back into the Mustang, and Alexander silently escorted me to my front steps.

"I'm sure he—" I began, but Alexander wasn't listening. Instead, he gave me a quick kiss on the lips. I opened the front door and reluctantly entered my house. I heard the sound of a car door slamming and a Mustang peeling away from the curb.

I struggled as usual to sleep. The only time I'd seen Alexander this upset was when we went to the SnowBall last winter and Trevor told him the only reason I liked him was that I thought he was a vampire. Instead of hanging out in bed, I sat on my desk and stared out my window.

I hoped I'd find Alexander resting against our tree or sitting on the swings. All I saw was a lonely maple and an empty swing set.

I replayed Sebastian's obsession with Becky over in my

mind. I imagined what would happen if Alexander and I were placed in a similar position.

Alexander was chasing me through the tombstones. The grass was wet with fresh rain, and the air filled with a gentle mist. I dodged a grave marker and then jumped over another as Alexander drew close. Fatigued yet exhilarated, I sprang over a third headstone. It caught the heel of my Mary Janes, I lost my balance, and I tumbled to the ground with a thud.

I felt a little stupefied. I sat up to find a sharp pain emanating from my right arm.

Alexander leaped to my aide. I raised my elbow. He held it softly.

"Is it broken?"

"Just bruised."

He blew off the dirt and gently picked the wet blades of grass from my skin and examined it closely. A large gash, the size of a pencil, raced up my forearm. We both watched as blood began to fill the slender wound.

"We are on sacred ground," I said, raising my wound toward his mouth.

Two fangs pierced through the break in his lips. He tried to cover them with the back of his hand.

"You need me as much as I need you," I said, pulling his hand away. "It's okay. You don't have to fight it anymore. You don't have to be strong."

I could see in his eyes that Alexander struggled, wondering what it would be like to finally taste my blood, as Sebastian had tasted Becky's.

"I'd still have to bite you. To turn you, like me."

"Perhaps it's time. We'd finally be together. Like I've always wanted. I've always needed you, Alexander."

"I need you too, Raven."

He took my arm and drew it up to his mouth. He closed his eyes, and I watched as he licked his lips and opened his mouth.

Suddenly, Nightmare jumped in front of the window and I was so startled, I was lucky I didn't fall off my desk and really bust my arm.

I wanted the reassurance that Alexander needed me just as much as I needed him. That he craved me, as Sebastian craved Becky. But I knew Alexander wasn't about to make that decision lightly. And did I want it, after all? I'd put so much of my thought into this magical and darkened world when right before me I was seeing vampires struggle with their lifestyle, as I struggled with mine.

At this point, I could only imagine Alexander biting me and taking me into his world. The fantasy of it thrilled me. I could only hope the reality, should it ever show itself, would be as good.

T he hours ticked away painfully slowly during school.
I was tormented as Becky raved incessantly about our
previous evening at Hooligans. She went on about how she
and Matt had a blast hanging out with the three of us, how
we all could be "best buds," and what a shame it was Sebastian was going to leave. She had no idea the evening had
ended with a nightmare—one caused by Sebastian. I was
in a fog all day. I couldn't get my mind off of Alexander
and Sebastian's falling-out. Did they make amends? Had
Sebastian left Dullsville? I begged for the sun to set as fast
as it could, but it seemed to toy with me as it hung over the
trees. When it lowered below the rooftops, I jumped on my
bike and took off. I had no idea what I might find when I
reached the Mansion.

The Mustang was still in the driveway, but the front

door of the Mansion was open.

"Jameson? Alexander?" I called. But no one answered.

The house was eerily quiet.

I scaled the main staircase and passed a half dozen rooms until I came to Sebastian's.

I tapped the door and it squeaked open.

The room was spotless. There were no signs that Alexander's best friend had even visited the Mansion. No coffin. No iPod, boxer shorts, or wallet. Not even a trace of Romanian dirt remained.

I felt as hollow as the empty room.

I ran throughout the Mansion. "Alexander!"

No response.

"Jameson?" I called.

The Creepy Man was nowhere in sight.

I entered the kitchen and found Alexander's best friend sitting alone at a rustic dinette, staring vapidly at a tiny plastic sword in his hand. His hair was unkempt, his eyelids droopy.

I stood for a moment. Sebastian wasn't talking. He didn't even acknowledge my presence.

I approached him tentatively.

"I'm sorry you're leaving," I finally said. "Apart from the fact that you want to break up my best friend and her boyfriend, we actually got along pretty well."

"Are you really?" he asked, gazing up at me.

"Sure. You brought light to the Mansion—literally," I teased.

But Sebastian didn't even smirk.

"Raven—what have I done? How could I have been so reckless—so selfish? A girl should never come between friends. I'm sorry things didn't turn out better than this."

"Alexander's still mad at you? I was hoping—"

"Not only didn't I find true love, I lost my best friend."

It pained me to see Sebastian hurting. He wasn't as controlled as Alexander, or as menacing as Jagger. But like all the vampires I'd met, he struggled with his place in the mortal world—just as I struggled.

"I'll talk to Alexander. I'm sure you'll be able to repair things—with some time. When are you heading back to Romania?"

"I'm not sure. . . . I can't return like this. What do I say to my parents? To his? I thought I might stay nearby for a few more days."

"Then you're not leaving town?" I was happy at the thought.

"I'm not sure. I might just take a few days to think things through. And figure out how to make amends."

"Does Alexander know?"

"We didn't talk much," he said with a nervous chuckle.

I pulled out a chair and sat by him. "Where are you going to stay?"

"I'm still not sure. . . ."

"Are you planning to crash in a hotel with a coffin?" I asked exasperatedly.

"I thought somewhere more obscure. In the woods—or perhaps in an old barn."

We both paused with dead concern.

"No—not that barn!" he corrected. "Not anywhere near that barn!" he said. "That's what has gotten me here in the first place."

For a moment I deliberated taking him into my house. But I knew it wouldn't work. Not only would I feel awkward getting in the middle of the two guys' feud, but how on earth could I hide his coffin bed?

"I'd invite you to my house . . . ," I said, wanting him to know I was trying to help, "but I think you might understand the massive complications in that plan."

"That's very kind of you—even after I did that to your friend? Well, both friends really . . ."

I sympathized with Sebastian's dilemma. He was a vampire—for better or for worse—and Alexander's best friend. If anyone knew his struggle, it had to be the gorgeous guy I was in love with.

"If you'll excuse me . . . ," I rose and backed out of the kitchen. "Alexander!" I called, running upstairs. Out of breath, I burst into Alexander's attic room.

I found my boyfriend sitting on his bed with a paintbrush in his hand.

On his easel was a beautiful painting of Alexander, me, and Sebastian. It was the very one he'd been working on so intently and that was bringing him so much joy. The one he'd never sell or auction off—the one that was created for only his possession.

"I guess I'm going to have to paint over him," he said.

"Don't you dare."

He had a quizzical look. "I thought you'd be . . ."

"Your best friend is downstairs, as upset as you are. You should understand him and his desires more than anyone."

"But I thought . . ."

"I can see that he doesn't have the same personality as you do. I know it's not easy for you to understand how impulsive he can be."

"Why do people think it's so easy for me, too?"

"It's not?" I prodded.

But Alexander didn't elaborate.

I held his hand. He was so strong yet so vulnerable at the same time. It pained me to see him struggle in any way, whether it was with the tribulations of being a vampire or the normal conflicts of anyone with emotions.

"I didn't say it was easy for either one of you. It's just the way you handle it. Becky is my best friend. . . . However, she's the total opposite of me in many ways. She would die before she'd ever confront anyone or defend herself. She is terrified of silly things like the dark and spiders and would rather visit a mall than a graveyard. I've protected her for years, like you've protected Sebastian with his loose lips and impulsive actions. But if I didn't have her—if she didn't stick by me, too—then I wouldn't have anyone."

Alexander folded his arms.

"Sebastian knows he messed up. But he's not going to leave Dullsville until he finds a way to reconcile with you. To me, that's a best friend."

"But I thought you'd be mad at him, too. After all, he was almost stalking Becky."

"I'm not happy about it. But your friendship is more important to him than she is. I want you to have a best friend just like I do, for better or for worse."

I waited as Alexander decided on his next move. He gazed at the picture he'd painted of the three of us together.

He stood up and placed the brush on the easel. He took my hand and led me downstairs.

We entered the kitchen, but it was empty of vampires. I followed Alexander outside, where Sebastian was loading his final bag into his trunk. Alexander left me on the steps and walked quickly to Sebastian. I winced, prepared to see fists and fangs fly.

I waited. And waited. And waited.

The two began talking. I was out of earshot, burning to know the contents of their conversation. At any moment, Sebastian was going to get in his car and drive off. I wasn't sure if I'd ever see him again. I wouldn't even get to say good-bye.

I felt a small pang in my stomach. I hated to see Alexander so upset with someone he cared about. I heard a car door close.

Just then, Alexander reached into the Mustang's trunk, put a duffel bag on his shoulder, and summoned his best friend. The two vampires returned toward the Mansion.

"Jameson," I called. "Prepare those smoothies with the tiny swords!"

I met Alexander at the Evans Park covered bridge the following night. The old pedestrian bridge was unused and unkempt. Wooden slatted shingles worn off over the years had gone unfixed. Paint had chipped away. Even the birds' nests were forgotten. I always thought the bridge was beautiful. A trickling creek ran beneath it and a tiny broken bench overlooked a dead bed of flowers. Tonight, however, I found the bridge decorated with twinkling yellow and white lights, which hung like sparkling icicles, making it a truly romantic and magical scene.

I crept inside to find a table with a flickering candelabra on it and two champagne glasses filled with soda.

Alexander emerged from the shadows, dreamy and gorgeous. I was breathless. There wasn't a place I'd rather be than in Alexander's presence. I rushed to him and squeezed him with all my might. It seemed like ages since we had been alone, and I planned to take advantage of our solitude. My fingers begged to touch his skin, to feel my boyfriend close, sense his breath against mine. His strong hands grasped my smaller ones and he intently kissed them, as if he, too, had missed our moments together. I gently stroked his face and ran my fingers over his lips, my black nail polish in striking contrast to his alabaster skin and pale red mouth.

Alexander and I had only a short time for our date. Becky was in the safe company of Matt and the soccer snobs at a scrimmage, and Jameson was doing his best to keep Sebastian entertained with a newly purchased Guitar Hero.

I curled up in Alexander's arms. The electricity between the two of us seemed unbreakable. When he kissed my neck, I wondered if it was as much a torture for him as it was for me.

Alexander had the power at any moment to turn me— whether I wanted him to or not. Was he thinking what it would be like to pierce his fangs into me and take my blood into his? But Alexander was thoughtful and cautious. If I were in the arms of another kind of vampire, perhaps like Jagger or Sebastian, I might have blood dripping down my neck. I wondered and admired how he could be so different.

"I don't know how you do it. Sebastian can't."

"It's not easy. I'm sitting with the most gorgeous girl I've ever seen in my life and she wants to be a vampire."

I melted at his compliment. "It seems easy to me. . . ."

I couldn't help but want to be bitten—if only to become a vampire before my best friend did.

A few pings of raindrops began to hit the roof of the bridge. A few moments later, it began to pour. It only added to our magically romantic night. I snuggled even closer to Alexander.

"Imagine it," I began. "We'd live in the Mansion together. I'd make you smoothies, and if we ran out—then you'd have me.

"We'd have a beautiful coffin together," I continued. "I'd decorate it with the most comfy pillows and blankets and tiny portraits that you'd paint of us. And we could wire it so we could listen to morbidly melodic music."

"I could take you to Romania and you could see my home," Alexander added. "We would dine outside on our balcony overlooking the twinkling city lights with my parents, and I'd take you into town and we'd dance until dawn."

I was excited by Alexander's enthusiasm. "You'd become a famous painter and I'd be an editor of a gothic magazine," I continued. "We'd travel to Paris for your showings and we'd attend gothic fashion shows. We'd hang out all night long and sleep all day."

"But you do that now," he joked.

"By myself. But if I were like you . . . we'd never have to be apart again," I said. "We'd be together, hidden away from the sunlight."

"And holding hands in the moonlight," he imagined.

"You'd never be alone. Not for a moment."

"Not for one moment?" he asked coyly.

"Well, maybe one. If you wanted some space."

"Forget it," he assured me. "I've been waiting for you all my life."

Alexander kissed me again.

"We wouldn't only have stolen moments like tonight," I urged. "We'd be together longer."

Raindrops continued to fall against the roof as he kissed my wrist. My vein showed prominently. Alexander's attention was drawn to my blue blood vessel.

"Are you ready?" I asked. "We're not on sacred ground, but we could go to the cemetery. We could finally be together."

Alexander paused. He stared deeply into my eyes, and so intently, I felt as if I were staring back into his soul. Then suddenly he turned away.

"It's not fair," I said, clasping my hands. "Sebastian wants to turn Becky and you don't want to turn me."

Alexander sat up. "First of all, he doesn't. He feels strongly for her—and now that he's crossed the line he's put all of us in jeopardy. He tasted her blood. He has a stronger pull to her than he already had."

It was a mistake to have brought up Sebastian. Now I'd distracted Alexander from his thoughts about me.

"I know," I said. "It's just that sometimes—"

"Raven, it's hard enough for me—with you, as we are right now."

I couldn't push him any further. I'd already spoiled his mood and the gorgeous night he'd created for me. I could tell he was just as concerned for Sebastian as he was for himself.

"I guess I shouldn't have let him in," he lamented.

"Are you kidding? He's your best friend. Sebastian is a sweetie," I reassured Alexander.

"He's much more impulsive than I am. Kind of like someone else I know," he said, lightening up.

"He's just fallen for the wrong girl," I said with a sigh.

"Then we have to find someone else for Sebastian to fall for," Alexander thought aloud.

"That's a great idea."

"He hasn't really had a steady girlfriend. Not only would this be helpful for Becky, but it would truly be helpful to him."

I was so touched—not only that Alexander was concerned for the welfare of my best friend, but that he felt such responsibility and loyalty for his own.

"Another mortal?" I asked. I thought about the Dullsvillian girls who had plagued me all my life. "There's a bunch of cheerleaders at school that I certainly wouldn't miss," I offered. "But on second thought, I refuse to let one of them be turned before I am."

"No," my boyfriend said. "She has to be a vampire."

"I'm afraid I'm short on vampire girls here," I said. But then I had a thought. "But in Hipsterville, there's a whole club full!"

Alexander lit up.

"I know two very eligible ones. Onyx and Scarlet. One

of them could be a perfect match!"

"How do we get them here?" he wondered aloud.

"That, I have no idea."

"Let's think. . . ."

"They are party girls," I said.

"Then we'll have a party."

"That's awesome! I love parties. Though truth be told, I haven't hosted many—or, in fact, any. No one would show up besides Becky."

"It will be a small, intimate gathering."

"Shall we have it at the cemetery?"

Alexander disagreed. "We'll have it at the Mansion. That way it will be discreet and no one will find out about it."

I gave Alexander a huge hug. I was excited to be hosting a party and thrilled at the prospect of seeing Scarlet and Onyx again.

"But how are we going to invite them?" he finally asked.

I reached into my purse and took out my cell phone. "I have them on speed dial."

After a few minutes of canoodling, I strolled outside the covered bridge to get more light from the streetlamp. I avoided a few puddles, as the rain had ceased.

I scrolled to Scarlet's contact number and pressed send. The line began to ring. And ring. And ring.

"Is she there?" Alexander asked impatiently.

I shook my head.

Just then, someone picked up. I could hear the pounding of loud music with overloaded bass in the background.

"Scarlet?" I said.

"Hello?" I barely heard her voice. "Hello?"

Then the phone went dead.

"I don't think she wants to speak to me," I said.

"I think she probably can't hear you. That club can be deafening."

"I'll try again."

I pushed redial and waited.

This time she picked up right away. "Raven, is that you?"

"Yes! Can you hear me?"

"Raven—is that you?"

"Yes!" I yelled.

"I think it's Raven—but I can't hear her," she said to someone.

"Scarlet? Onyx? Are you there?"

The call was dropped. All I heard was my own voice shouting.

"I guess we'll have to try later," Alexander said, resigned. He wiped off the damp bench with a tissue he had in his pocket and sat down.

"If she can't hear my invite, then maybe she can see it."

"What do you mean?"

I sat down next to Alexander and texted as fast as I could. He peered over my shoulder, curious.

Onyx and Scarlet—
Mansion Mayhem!
Mansion on top of Benson Hill only a few towns away.
Saturday Night @ Sunset
Raven

"Now what?" he asked.

"We wait."

"How long?"

"If she sees the message, it could be within a minute. If she doesn't, it could take days."

"We don't have days."

"I know. . . ."

We sat in silence, his arm around me, my cell phone in my lap. We both were zoned out when we heard a few beeps. I showed Alexander my phone.

Can't W8 2 party w/u!
X,
S & O

Alexander gave me a huge squeeze, and we spent the rest of the evening pressed against each other's black and pale red lips.

The party at the Mansion was going to have to be top secret. I couldn't even invite Becky and Matt. I hated having an intimate party and not inviting my best friend. However, I had to remind myself of the motivation for the party—to get Sebastian's mind off Becky and onto a vampire girl.

Becky and I sat at a side entrance to the school, she intently eating her lunch on a step while I was perched on a half wall, doodling a macabre party in my notebook.

A figure stood next to me. "What's that?" Trevor said, snatching my notebook.

"Wouldn't you like to know."

"It looks like a sketch for a funeral."

"And if you're lucky—or rather, I am—you could be the guest of honor." I tried swiping it back, but he held it out of reach.

"You and your friends are having some gathering where you try to bring back the dead—"

"We call it a party," I said back to him.

"A party? And when should I be there?" he asked.

"A party? Who's having a party?" Becky asked, placing her trash into her brown lunch bag.

"Uh, no one. Trevor's just mouthing off."

"Well, your sketch looked exactly like a party to me."

"There isn't a party—not now, not ever! C'mon, Becky, let's go. This location is suddenly very unappetizing."

Trevor remained at the half wall, puzzled, as Becky and I escaped into school.

Sebastian and Alexander were hanging out in the gazebo when I arrived.

"We're going to have a party," I said to Sebastian.

"I know, Alexander told me all about it. I do appreciate the lengths you guys are going to to repair my broken heart," he said dramatically, his hand over his chest.

"You never know where you might meet the perfect person," I said.

"Listen, I've been traveling all my life and I haven't found her yet. Well, I thought I had, but I've resigned myself to my fate. Becky will marry Matt and I'll be alone for eternity."

Alexander and I were chuckling at his histrionics when we heard the sound of a car coming up the Mansion's long driveway.

"Are the guests arriving already?" Sebastian asked sarcastically.

No one drove up to the haunted-looking Mansion at night, and I didn't recognize the car. The three of us headed back inside through the kitchen and waited in the dining room as Jameson answered the door.

"I'm Giles Lunken with the *Gazette*," we heard a voice say.

Giles Lunken? He was a well-known writer throughout Dullsville who had a column showcasing local and international talent.

"I was wondering if I could speak with Alexander Sterling," he continued.

"May I ask what this is regarding?" Jameson asked like a strict butler.

"Is he the artist that painted the canvases sold in last month's auction? We were thinking of doing an article about him for the *Gazette*. He's so young—it's amazing he's so talented. Also, I'd love to come back with my photographer."

"I'm afraid that's impossible."

"Why?" His voice was accusatory. "He's not the artist?"

"Uh . . . You will have to come back at another time."

"Then it was another artist?" Mr. Lunken prompted.

"I'm not saying that," Jameson answered firmly.

"Then what are you saying? Did he paint those paintings?"

"Of course he did—"

"Then does he have a personal phone or cell number?" Mr. Lunken pulled out a PDA.

"I'm afraid he doesn't."

"An e-mail?" Mr. Lunken questioned.

"No."

"He doesn't have e-mail?"

Jameson shook his bald head.

"Does he have a Web site? I couldn't find any information on him."

"You can leave your card with me," Jameson suggested.

"Uh . . . I don't have one."

"You don't have a card?" Jameson asked. "Interesting . . ."

I couldn't help but snicker. Alexander put his hand gently over my mouth.

"I'll come back in a few days."

"That would be best."

Jameson passed us, and Alexander gave him the thumbs-up sign. The Creepy Man headed for the kitchen as we settled in the living room. Sebastian plopped down on the antique sofa.

"Dude!" Sebastian said with an impressed tone. "You are famous. Soon we'll have to invest in a security system to weed out the paparazzi."

"Funny," Alexander said. "Shouldn't we have heard his car take off by now?"

Sebastian leaned back and peeked out the worn velvet curtain.

"He didn't leave."

Alexander and I jumped onto the sofa and the three of us peered out.

Giles's car was still in the driveway, but he was nowhere to be found. He soon emerged from the side of the Mansion with a notepad. He continued walking, staring up at the attic window. Finally, he examined the Mustang, jotting down a few notes. Several minutes later, there was a knock at the door.

Sebastian fingered his dreadlocks, straightened his shirt, and opened the door.

"Alexander?" we heard Mr. Lunken say.

"No, I'm Mr. Sterling's assistant."

"I was just here a moment ago—speaking with an older gentleman. And I noticed a light in the upstairs window and this car . . . I just thought . . ."

"He has a very busy schedule," Sebastian said.

"I can do the story without your help."

Sebastian paused. "Fine. I think we can work you in. He'll meet you at Javalicious—"

"I'd like to meet here," the reporter insisted.

Sebastian turned to Alexander, who shook his head adamantly.

"Please come back in two days after sunset."

"After sunset?" Giles asked.

"I mean early evening. He'll be waiting." Sebastian closed the door.

"What are you doing?" Alexander asked. "We already discussed that I need to remain private. It would be dire to have a reporter see the real Mansion and discover the real me."

"Then he won't meet the real you—or the real Mansion.

But we can't put him off. He could write anything."

"So what is your big plan?"

"He was snooping around anyway—who knows what he might say on his own. We have to show him you're just like everyone else. Mortal."

"But you've invited him here. And why in two days? We might as well get it over with."

"He doesn't need to see the whole house. Just the first floor."

"Have you seen the first floor?" I said. "It would make a ghost scream."

Sebastian thought for a moment. "Not when it gets a Sebastian Camden makeover. It will look like everyone else's home. And you won't be bothered again."

Alexander's stern mood quickly lightened up.

"There's a reason he's my best friend," he said, slapping his arm around Sebastian's shoulder.

Creepy Man and Monster Girl

Mom—I need you!" I declared when Alexander dropped me off at my house. "Where are you?"

I found my parents sitting in the family room. My mom was finishing a scrapbook and my dad was channel surfing.

"I need your help—" I continued.

"I already gave you your allowance," my mother said, gluing a border on a photograph.

"I don't need money."

"I'm not signing a note asking for you to be dismissed early because you want to watch *Dark Shadows*. I told you to DVR it."

"Mom. This is way important."

"Are you suspended?" she asked.

"No."

"Expelled?"

I shook my head.

"Arrested?"

I folded my arms in disgust. "Are you finished?"

"I'm all ears," my mom said.

"Alexander needs some new furniture for the Mansion."

"Hmm . . . I suppose you want something Victorian? You never know what you might find at a yard sale."

"We don't have time to wait for the weekend."

"How about Annie's Antiques?"

"No, we're doing a makeover. We need to make the Mansion look like our home. Or the neighbors'. Or the Mitchells'."

My dad came out of his TV coma. "What's going on?"

"Raven needs some tips on making the Mansion appear more . . . normal. She wants it to look more like our home."

My father was confused. "Our home? But we don't have bats."

"Or spiderwebs," my mom said.

"Or creaking floors," my dad added.

"We do have those upstairs," my mom corrected.

"That's true."

"Are you through?" I asked, disgusted with my parents' teasing. "This has to be done immediately. Where are all your catalogs?"

"Why all of a sudden do you want to do this makeover?" my mom asked.

"Alexander is going to have an interview."

"How exciting," she replied.

But I wasn't as thrilled. "Once the reporter sees what the Mansion looks like, Alexander will be the laughingstock of this town."

"I hardly think that will happen."

"You just did it yourself. You both were making fun of it. How will he feel . . . with some reporter's comments published throughout town?"

For once I had silenced my parents.

"See our problem?" I asked.

"Your father and I were just kidding. You're right—we really shouldn't have said those things."

"But the town—they won't be fooling around. They'll mean it. You see how I've been treated for years."

"That's what I don't understand," my dad said. "I thought you were all about being yourself—no matter what."

"I am."

"Then I figured Alexander would be, too."

"Of course he is," I said emphatically.

"There is no reason, then," my mom said, "that Alexander should change who he is—or where he lives."

She had a point.

"So where is our nonconforming daughter?" my dad asked. "What has happened to you?"

We don't want the whole town to know my boyfriend's a vampire. That he sleeps in a coffin and has a cellar filled with bottles of blood, okay? I wanted to say.

I was on trial in front of my parents. They waited for

the accused to speak—to declare if I was guilty of trading in my own belief system. I was asking them to understand why I was changing my whole character in order to impress the very town from which I'd been an outcast my entire life.

They were correct. Under normal circumstances, I'd never go along with Alexander trying to change who he was. But if the town knew he was a vampire, he'd be the one in danger.

"Maybe Alexander doesn't want the town to see his real image," I began.

"Why?" my mom asked.

"It's an invasion of his space."

"How do you figure that?"

"The Mansion is his studio, his home, his family. He's already shared his soul in his paintings—does he have to share it in a newspaper, too?"

My parents agreed. I was beginning to get through to them.

"Besides, it's not my decision," I said. "It's Alexander's. And he wants the Mansion to appear like any other home in Dullsville."

My mother's bewilderment turned to joy. "Then I guess I'm forced to help you shop."

"Jameson and I are going to pick up the furniture after school. I just don't know where to begin, and I thought you'd be great in giving me some ideas."

"Come into my private stash." I followed my mom into her bedroom.

Where a man might have stashed *Playboy*s, my mom had hidden her *Pottery Barn*s. She reached underneath her bed and pulled out a large plastic container.

"I have every issue from every home store."

We hunkered down on her bed like two girls at a sleepover. We spread out the catalogs and pored over the slick pages.

"Rugs are a great accent. Framed pictures can make a statement. Clocks can really be striking." She noted pages with Post-its, and with a thick black marker I circled items that reminded me of Trevor's home.

"I was hoping for a day like this since you were a little girl," she said, "for decorating your room—but I'll settle for decorating Alexander's."

Jameson and I were armed with catalogs and a credit card. We had to go to the one place I'd never imagined the Creepy Man would ever escort me to—the mall.

It was an understatement to say that we were an odd pair. Elderly mall walkers, tweens with cell phones and Vera Bradley backpacks, kissing couples, and families filled the food court. There was only one bald butler and morbidly dressed girl.

We entered a home store I'd only been in when I was being dragged by my mother and the mall benches were already occupied.

We were immediately confronted by a friendly woman with a rock star headset. "Do you need help?" she asked sincerely.

"You could say that," I said. "We'd like to purchase a few things for the home."

Her forehead wrinkled as she tried to assess the couple who stood before her. Uncle and niece? Father and daughter? Boyfriend and young girlfriend?

By the expression on her face, I think she settled for Creepy Man and Monster Girl.

"It's not for my home," I reassured her. "It's for his home."

"All right, then." The saleswoman did her best to hide her discomfort.

"Miss . . . ?" Jameson asked.

"Lauren."

"Miss Lauren," he began in a soft and velvety Romanian accent, "I am so delighted that you will be helping us. I can tell you have impeccable taste."

Lauren was immediately captured by the Creepy Man's compliment. "Thank you," she gushed.

"And, Miss Lauren, we need to have these delivered quickly," Jameson told her.

"If it's in stock, we can have it delivered the next day."

"Then lead me to those items," he said.

Lauren guided us around the store like a docent in a fine arts museum.

We picked out a few rugs, a desk and hutch, and furniture covers. She showed us a dozen lamps and pushed one long hanging rug after another until Jameson found one he liked.

I had a blast shopping with the Creepy Man. My mom

usually took ages to decide between two varieties of the same item, then, after deciding on the most perfect one, went to another store, only to finally come back to the original and buy it, while Jameson instantaneously picked out furniture, rugs, and accessories.

Lauren rang up our purchases and Jameson handed over his credit card and signed his name.

We left the store with oversized shopping bags like any other normal Dullsvillian.

Now all we needed was a cleaning company.

Alexander wouldn't let me inside until the Mansion's makeover was complete. I heard bustling and tried to peek into the window, but the dirt blocked my view.

I was seated on the stoop when I received a text.

Hey Hottie, What are you doing?

The sender was from an unavailable number. I dismissed the call, and as I waited on the stoop, the Mansion's door finally creaked open.

Alexander stood as I'd never seen him before. He was wearing pressed jeans and an oxford shirt, a brown leather belt and shiny loafers. He was unbearably handsome.

"Where is Alexander?" I asked.

"What do you think?" he asked, nervous about my response.

"You are gorgeous! I'd never imagined you as an 'insider,'" I said, checking him out. "You look like you belong in a prep school."

"Good, that's the look we're going for."

The Mansion had been transformed into a spread from *Homes & Gardens*. Everything seemed completely wrong. With the new slipcovers, the couches appeared brand new and the room clean, sweet-smelling, and free of any unwanted eight-legged insects. Hurricane lamps and framed flowers lined the mantel. Bright yellow and white pillows popped out against white linen-covered chairs.

"It looks like someone else lives here," I said.

"You think so?" Sebastian asked, pleased with the results. "Alexander will be like any other person living in town—only he'll have a butler instead of a few parents. That will accentuate his trust-fund status," he said, thinking out loud.

"You've covered all your bases," I said, noticing that a floor-length candelabra had been replaced with a silver floor lamp. "Giles Lunken won't have anything to say, except 'He's one of our own.'"

"And," Sebastian began, "it gets better. Now there's no need for a photographer."

I followed Sebastian into a room—formerly the parlor, now a studio with desk, computer, and easel.

"It's almost finished. I just have to print it out," he said.

Sebastian went to the printer tray and handed me a glossy photo. I held it in my hand.

It was a picture of Alexander!

"This will be his artist's headshot," Sebastian boasted.

I was amazed. For the first time in my life, I held a picture of my vampire boyfriend. "I love it! It looks exactly like you!"

"I used one of my image-enhancement software programs," Sebastian proudly said, "and played around with some photographs I found online. I used Johnny Depp and made a few tweaks to bone structure and added pale skin, and *voilà*! Alexander."

"It looks like a real photograph. And it looks like you! Can I keep it?"

"We have to give it to Mr. Lunken for the article. But I can print you another one."

"Print a hundred!" I ordered.

I was so distracted by finally possessing a photograph of Alexander, I almost forgot that the preppy guy standing in front of me was him.

My boyfriend tugged at the collar of his shirt and fiddled with his shoes. I watched him as he uncomfortably tried to adapt to his new image. He was trying his best to fool even himself.

We returned to the living room, where he put a log in the fireplace.

"You hate it, don't you," I said.

"This house is beautiful—don't get me wrong," he lamented. "And the clothes look great on a guy in a magazine. . . . But . . ."

"What?"

"I don't want to let you down."

"Me?" I said. "I've spent my whole life not conforming. Why would I judge you if you don't feel comfortable in an image that isn't your own?"

"Because if I don't do it—if that reporter snoops

around or it slips out that I sleep in a coffin . . . that I drink blood for breakfast . . ." Alexander's voice rose. "It is dangerous not only for me, but for you."

"I understand." I, too, was afraid Mr. Lunken would find out and reveal Alexander's true identity. But mostly for Alexander's sake.

"I'm not sure you do. . . . Is this the life you really want, Raven? The one you've desired all your life? Or is it just about the fantasy of it?"

"What do you mean?" I asked. Being a vampire had always fascinated me. I knew there were drawbacks, but weren't there drawbacks to being mortal?

"You are all about showing the world who you truly are. What if you couldn't anymore?" he asked sincerely.

It was something I hadn't thought about. I'd imagined a life of darkness and mystery, but not one where I'd have to hide who I was. "I don't know. . . ."

"Think about it. Me, Sebastian, Jagger, even Luna. We're all in a club that no mortal wants to join—except for you."

"But—"

"Have you even told your own mother about me? Or Becky?"

"Of course not. I thought you didn't . . ."

"I know. I don't." He wandered back to the mantel, stoked the fire, and gazed into the crackling flames shooting from the burning logs. "But sometimes I do."

I was speechless. Alexander was so much more complicated than I could ever imagine. I did feel sorry for him.

I never hid from others my thoughts and tastes, no matter how outlandish, and yet he had to keep secret everything about his lifestyle.

"Sometimes I want your parents to know," he continued. "Just be able to be who I am. And not have them be fearful of me. Not have them run away."

I couldn't imagine my parents running from Alexander under any circumstances. Maybe this was my opportunity to let them into his world.

"Do you want me to tell them?" I moved toward him and drew him in to me.

"It will be the end of everything—of our relationship, of my living here."

"What if it isn't?" I asked excitedly. "What if they embrace it? Then neither one of us would have to hide it anymore."

"You think your father wants you dating a vampire? A guy who drinks blood to exist?"

"They're former hippies. They might think they were having a flashback."

"I'm serious. They aren't hippies anymore. They are parents of a teenage girl."

"Well . . ."

He sat down on the sofa. "It's been great having Sebastian here. And you. It's been a long time since I've been able to be myself, apart from being with you."

It was quite the sight—Alexander, my once gothic prince, transformed into a handsome quarterback from a boarding school, living in a palatial mansion, pained with loneliness even as I sat right next to him.

"This is my life, Raven, whether I have to hide out in a Mansion, live among my kind, or hide out in the Dungeon at the Coffin Club. It's all about secrecy and survival."

I'd never been about hiding or not getting in people's faces. Maybe I couldn't be a vampire after all. Could I take the solitude? Or wandering around like Sebastian, trying to find those who were like me?

I felt Alexander was pushing me away—not from him, but from the fantasy of being a vampire. So if I was to truly be with him, I'd have to show him how much I cared for him and push back.

"But we'd live together," I said. "Like your parents do. I just want to be with you—and I just want everyone to love you for who you are, just like I do. But I understand . . . Alexander, I know I'm impulsive, but I want what's best for you—no matter what that means."

He turned to me, his eyes soulful and his shiny hair glistening. A gorgeous smile emerged from his serious face.

I fixed his collar so it rested flatly. "Besides, it is only temporary. But don't be mad at me if I slip and call you Trevor."

Alexander didn't find my joke amusing, and he rose.

"I didn't mean to—" I started.

He didn't speak but shook his head.

"I'm sorry. I was just teasing."

"No—you're right. This isn't how I live. And most important, this isn't who I am. He unbuttoned his shirt and removed it, exposing a white Cure T-shirt.

I was startled and elated by his bravado. I ran to him and gave him a squeeze so hard I thought I'd pushed the air out of him.

"Jameson, we have some moving to do," he called.

Sebastian and Jameson entered the room.

"We're returning the Mansion and me to our original state," Alexander declared.

"What happened?" Sebastian asked.

"It's just not me. I don't have to come out and say I'm a vampire, but on the other hand, I also don't have to be ashamed of being myself."

"So what do you want to do now?" Jameson asked.

"Reschedule the interview. We're going to return the furniture. Immediately."

"All of it?" Sebastian asked.

Alexander nodded.

Jameson shuffled over to Alexander. "Can we at least keep this rug?"

Alexander smiled. "Of course."

"And my desk?" Sebastian pleaded.

"Yes. . . ."

"Can we keep that outfit?" I whispered, coyly tugging at his brown leather belt. "Just for fun?"

"Fine!" he reconciled. "But everything else goes back. I have an interview to do!"

The next day after sunset, I bounded over to the Mansion with a renewed sense of delight. I was eager to see the Mansion return to normal—or what Dullsvillians called a nightmare. I was proud that Alexander made the decision to be himself—or at least be as real as he could be without putting his true identity in danger. I knew it was an extremely hard choice for him to make—but either way he was going to be in the story. It was ultimately better that he shared the macabre artist that he was rather than an untrue, khaki-clad version of what he thought the town wanted him to be.

When I arrived atop Benson Hill, the Mansion's door was wide open.

I entered the foyer to find the Mansion restored to its original disorder. The scent of lit candles and musty air that I'd grown to love wafted through the halls. The brand-new crisp white linen covers were gone, exposing the worn Victorian couches. The silver floor lamps had been replaced with dripping candelabras. And the freshly purchased easel and metal desk with blue locker drawers had been taken from the library and the old desk and library books returned.

Curious, I bolted up the grand staircase. I peeked into Jameson's room to find his new accent rug at the foot of his bed. When I surveyed Sebastian's room, the only thing organized was his shiny new desk.

As I drew closer to the TV room, I heard Alexander and Sebastian talking intently.

"So haven't you thought about it, man?" Sebastian asked. "You must have."

"Of course I have," Alexander answered.

"Isn't it difficult to resist? She is beautiful."

"It isn't easy."

What were they talking about—who were they talking about? I pressed my back flat to the wall and did my best to hear.

"She isn't a vampire," Alexander said.

"But if she was—man, you could be living the dream. You could sell the bottles in your cellar. She'd quench your thirst for eternity."

They both laughed.

"I agree with you that it would be easier if she had been born into our world," Sebastian began. "That's what I think. Then there are no decisions—no conflicts, no pressure."

"It's enormous. I try my best not to think about it."

"But you do—"

"Of course I do."

I waited with bated breath to finally get a glimpse into Alexander's thoughts. Ones that I knew he was reluctant to tell me about.

"If Becky were to go out with me, what would I do?" Sebastian pondered. "It would be very hard for me not to want to turn her. How do you manage?"

I waited an eternity for Alexander's response. I pressed my ear closer to the door. I, like Sebastian, was eager to know how Alexander managed.

"It's difficult."

"If only she were born a vampire," Sebastian said again, "then it would be easier."

"Then she wouldn't be Raven," Alexander lamented.

I sighed. But what did Alexander think about turning me? I was dying to know more.

"So . . . ," Sebastian pressed. "What's keeping you from it?"

Alexander paused. "Not Raven," I heard him say. "Not my love for her. Or us being together."

I smiled inside and out.

"I do imagine that moment," Alexander continued. "Raven and I together on sacred ground. The first time I laid eyes on her, I knew she was what I'd been searching for. What I didn't find with Luna or any girl I'd ever known. But I never planned to fall for a mortal—the responsibility of it all. But no one said love is easy."

I tried my best not to scream in delight. Listening to

Alexander admit to Sebastian that he truly wanted me in his world was what I'd been waiting for.

"Do you think you ever will?" Sebastian asked. "Ask her . . ."

Would Alexander really turn me? I waited for his answer, but all I heard was deafening silence.

"Miss Raven!" I heard a voice say from the shadows.

I thought I'd jump clear through the Mansion's roof.

"I didn't know you arrived," the Creepy Man said in his thick Romanian accent. "You must have snuck in."

"The door was wide—"

"Raven?" Alexander called from the room. Suddenly he was standing before me.

"Uh . . . ," he stammered. "I didn't know you were here. . . ." It was obvious he was calculating in his head whether I'd heard their conversation.

Sebastian was sitting with a gaming guitar in his hand.

"Sebastian was just going to show off his guitar talents," Alexander said, changing the subject. "We're just missing a gothic rock star."

"Uh . . . yeah . . . ," Sebastian said. "I could use a singer."

They both looked to me.

"Sure," I said. "Just as long as you both have earplugs."

The following day, Alexander closed the coffin lid on Sebastian's and my participation in his interview. We were banished from the Mansion, and just to be safely at a distance Sebastian and I met at Dullsville's fountain until Alexander could join us.

It was odd, to say the least, to be hanging out with Alexander's best friend without Alexander. What were we going to talk about? Would it be strange to be hanging out with a guy who wasn't my boyfriend? The only other guy I was ever alone with, besides the occasional run-in with Trevor, was my snarky little brother.

There was no doubt Sebastian was charming. His mood was playful and his intentions toward me benign.

What I didn't plan on was anyone seeing us, since there was a soccer game at school and the whole town was going to be there.

"Raven," I heard a sweet voice call. "Are you two on a date?"

It was Becky, the last person, besides Trevor, I wanted Sebastian to see.

"Hey, what are you doing here?" I asked. "I thought you'd be at school, cheering for Matt."

"I'm on my way. Where's Alexander?"

"He has an interview with the *Gazette*. So I was being the tour guide—only Sebastian's already seen everything in town."

"I know one thing you haven't seen: Our school's winning soccer team. Wanna come?"

"We can't," I said.

"Have you ever seen a soccer game?" Becky asked naively.

"Yes—" Sebastian replied.

"Well, you haven't seen Matt play."

"True," he said, "but I'm not sure that's a good idea. We're supposed to meet Alexander in an hour."

Even Sebastian tried to put off my best friend.

"Don't be a stick-in-the-mud. I can bring you back here in time."

"You know how I feel about soccer," I said, trying to be diplomatic. "And especially going to school when I don't have to."

"Oh, it will be fun. There aren't any tombstones, but you're sure to see a killer match."

Before I knew it, Becky was playfully leading Sebastian toward her truck. He looked to me for help. He was struggling with her touching him, and he was doing his best not to make eye contact with her.

She opened the passenger door and Sebastian reluctantly began to get in.

"No—I'll sit in the middle," I insisted, squeezing in before Sebastian had the chance to sit down.

I didn't want Sebastian to be too close to Becky. He'd tasted her blood. That meant Sebastian felt even more of a draw to Becky than he had originally. I could see him wrestling with his inner vampire.

Sebastian stared out the window. Becky did her best to engage him in conversation, and he did his best to be polite but remain uninterested.

"Don't leave me alone with her," Sebastian pleaded as he and I sat on the bleachers. Becky was at the refreshment stand while we held a seat for her. "Alexander will kill me if he finds out I'm seeing her again. You know I didn't plan this."

"I know—neither did I. We could both get in trouble."

Becky returned with some chips and a container holding three drinks. She handed the tray to me, and as I reached for it, she sat down in between us. Sebastian scooted away.

He took out his cell phone and began texting.

"Want some chips?" she asked him.

He fiercely shook his head.

"Who are you texting?"

"Just some girls," he said.

Becky dismissed him and took her drink and chips.

There was a time-out in the game.

I received a text again from an unavailable number.

I know where you are . . .

"Who's texting you?" Becky asked. "I'm here, and I'm the only one who you text."

"I'm not sure. I think they have the wrong number."

The soccer snobs returned to the field.

"How long is this going to be?" Sebastian asked with an obnoxiously audible yawn.

"What's wrong with him?" Becky whispered to me. "He's acting very strangely."

"I'm not sure. . . ."

Just then Trevor scored a goal and the fans erupted in cheers. Sebastian rose to see what was going on.

"We're winning," she said.

Sebastian and Becky locked gazes. They both sat down,

and he put away his phone.

Before long, Sebastian had lowered his guard. He was into the game, rooting for Matt, and glowing at Becky.

He took out his cell phone and began snapping pictures of the action. Then he focused it on Becky, who began to get caught up in Sebastian's enthusiasm. She posed while I sat as inert as a tombstone.

"C'mon, Rave—" she said, placing her arm around me.

"Yes, Raven, I'd like some of you, too," Sebastian suggested.

I couldn't even muster a fake smile.

"Now let me take one of you," Becky said, retrieving her phone.

"No—I hate being photographed." Sebastian shielded his face with the drink tray.

"Weird. Alexander does, too," Becky said. "Must be something in the water in Romania."

"Must be," I said.

"Then how am I going to remember you when you leave?" she asked, snatching the tray from him.

Sebastian froze. His soft, lovelorn eyes melted even more. Becky's comments had pierced his already aching heart.

"All right," he said.

He gazed into the camera intently. He smiled adoringly at Becky. She snapped her camera and the flash went off. He winced as if he'd been struck by a soccer ball.

"Are you all right?" she asked.

"I got something in my eye . . . ," he said, recovering his composure.

She tucked her phone into her purse and turned her attention back to the game, unaware that she had unwittingly broken his heart. She could never possess his image and he could never possess her love.

Becky waved wildly to Matt just as the buzzer went off.

"Final quarter," she said.

"We have to meet Alexander," I said. "We need to go."

Off in the distance, a shadowy figure emerged over the horizon and began strolling down the grassy hill toward us.

Even from a distance, his presence was intense. A figure like no other. My own breath escaped me and I felt a magnetic and magical connection. For a moment, words eluded me.

Handsome, charismatic, and truly alluring. Alexander Sterling, the perfect vampire.

Paper Chase

I stumbled into the kitchen, my vision blurry from lack of sleep and caked-on eyeliner that had smeared like a chocolate bar in the summer heat.

I was greeted by my overly chipper parents, nursing their coffee and tea before making their way to work.

"I bet this will wake you up," my mom said, finding me bumping into the counter as I reached for a mug. "Alexander's in the paper!"

My eyelids shot open like a rocket.

"Where is it?" I scoured the countertop and dinette. "Do you have it?"

"I think Billy read it last."

"Billy? You let Billy touch it?" I was horrified. "How could you! I know he got his snotty paws all over it! He probably mangled the whole thing!"

"Calm down," my father said.

I stormed upstairs to find my brother's door locked. I banged so hard, my fist pulsed with pain.

"It'll cost you," I heard him yell back.

"It will cost you—an arm and a leg!"

The door slowly opened and I pushed myself inside. Billy was nowhere to be found. I jerked open his closet door, then heard his nerdy little voice from behind me.

"He says he sleeps in a coffin!" he teased.

"What?"

I spun around. Billy was standing at his door with the *Gazette* in his smarmy little hand.

I'm not sure who took off first. We both tore down the stairs as Billy cried, "Mom, she's trying to kill me!"

"Nerd Boy—" I screeched, as I'd done all his life.

I hadn't called him that name in months, but in my anger it just naturally rang out.

I tackled him before he reached the kitchen. I tried to wrangle the paper out of his hand as he pleaded with my parents for help.

It had been a while since we had a major sibling blowout bodyslam event, and he had grown stronger. It took all my might to hold him at bay.

"Raven, get off him," my dad shouted.

"Billy, give your sister the paper!" my mom ordered.

"She's sitting on my chest!" Billy hollered.

My dad pulled me off my brother by my woven belt, and I grabbed the paper from his hand.

I took off for my room, locked the door behind me, and hopped onto my bed. I spread out the paper and carefully tried to smooth the wrinkles.

Staring back at me on the front page of the Arts section was my boyfriend, with the caption "An Artist Amongst Us."

"He is so handsome!" I cheered.

OUR TOWN'S BEST-KEPT SECRET. A budding young artist, hiding out on Benson Hill.

I'd always heard ghost stories about the Mansion on Benson Hill, but I didn't see any spirits wandering through the halls. I was invited into an old-fashioned estate with a reclusive teen. Homeschooled his whole life, Alexander spends his days and nights painting.

"What is his inspiration?" I asked him.

"A girl named Raven," he replied.

Though I only saw the first floor, the rest of the Mansion appeared the same. He claims to sleep in a coffin and have a wine cellar straight from Transylvania. This artist might as well be a writer, too. But this interviewer wasn't fooled. The only thing he was really hiding was his talent. Though Alexander Sterling may be able to spin a yarn, he is also able to paint.

There is more to this artist than could ever be told. It has to be seen. All you need to do is take a look at one of his paintings. You can see how he loves this town and the people who inhabit it.

"Do you want to be famous? Like Picasso, Dalí—Monet?" I asked him.

"No," he said. "I just want to be like—me."

I riffled through my desk and found some tape. I placed my boyfriend's article right over my headboard.

Even wrinkled, Alexander Sterling was still the most gorgeous guy I'd ever seen.

I wasn't the only one who read the article on Alexander. In a town the size of Dullsville, small as a Shrinky Dink, any news was news. No one wanted to be left out from any new information or, worse, be the last one to know.

A group of cheerleaders was stretching out in the hallway while I waited for Becky outside the restroom. I was exhausted as usual.

"Did you see the picture of that Mansion guy?" the captain asked.

"He's totally hot," her assistant said, fixing her headband.

"He's really funny," another said.

"Did you see how he was ribbing the reporter? He must be really confident to do that."

"And talented. My parents bought one of his pictures at the Art Auction a few months ago," the captain boasted.

"Hot, talented, and funny."

"How did *she* ever land him?" her assistant said.

They all glared at me. Just then I received a text.

Funny article.

Picture of a vampire?

Impossible.

It was pitch-black when I went to Becky's house to meet her. Her parents weren't home and her house was unlocked. I called her name throughout each room, but she didn't answer. I knew she was afraid to go to the barn alone, but perhaps she needed to replace the rake. I found the flashlight resting on the back-porch railing.

"Becky? Where are you?"

When I finally reached the barn, the metal door was ajar.

"Becky? Are you in there?"

I heard some whispering voices and a giggle.

"Becky? Is that you? Are you okay?"

I shined the light on a few bales of hay. On an empty ladder. Then the tractor. It caught Becky, who quickly covered her face.

"Becky, what are you doing in here? You hate the dark."

Her hair was messy and she bore a menacing smirk on her face. I helped her up when I noticed two fresh wounds on her neck.

"No! What has Sebastian done to you?"

"What are you and Alexander waiting for?"

"No—Becky! What about Matt?"

"He's not a vampire!"

Just then I heard a beeping sound. I awoke to find Mrs. Hathaway and a classroom full of students staring at me.

"Miss Madison," she said with a stern voice. "Is that a cell phone I heard?"

"No—it was my alarm clock."

The class laughed.

"I have the authority to confiscate anything that is electronic, other than a calculator—which, I might add, you don't need in history class."

Mrs. Hathaway returned to her lesson, and I quickly checked my message.

Let's make history together.

I glanced up and saw Trevor peering back at me.

I shook off my dream, and Mrs. Hathaway stepped out of class.

"What are you doing this weekend," Becky asked, "besides sleeping?"

Alexander's party was fast approaching. I didn't have much time to decorate. I only had one day to gather some gothic and groovy items. I'd been so distracted with keeping Sebastian away from Becky that I hadn't had much time to be excited about Onyx and Scarlet's arrival or figure out something to wear.

"Uh . . . not sure," I finally answered.

"Why don't we all get together?"

"I think Alexander has plans," I said truthfully.

"Doing what?"

"I'm not sure. I just think I heard him say he was doing something. Nothing big—just hanging in."

"We can stay in, too . . . unless you don't want us over."

"Oh . . . it's not that. I just hate for you to cancel something dreamy like a movie night when all we are doing is hanging out playing video games."

"Matt loves gaming. Besides, he's never been inside the Mansion. And I haven't either, for that matter. We were only outside for Alexander's 'Welcome to the Neighborhood' party."

"How about I get back to you?"

I waited for Becky's response.

"Okay. Text me when you know," she finally said.

I felt awful keeping Becky in the dark about Alexander's party. She was my best friend—I included her in everything. For that matter, she was the only one I'd ever included. If it wasn't for Becky, I'd have been totally alone all of my life. This was the thanks she got—being excluded from an intimate gathering hosted at the Mansion. But I had to remind myself of the reason I was having the party in the first place—to keep her safe and mortal.

I was really shaken by my dream. Imagining Becky as a vampire—and how much she enjoyed it—jolted me. I liked my best friend just the way she was.

But the dream felt so real. The fact that my best friend became a vampire before I became one haunted me. I was struck—by jealousy. No one in this town wanted to be a vampire more than I did. Not Becky, or a Pradabee, or an unsuspecting soccer snob. If anyone was going to be bitten in this town, it was going to be me.

When the final bell rang, marking my freedom from the doldrums of Dullsville High, I met Becky at our lockers. "Do you mind dropping me off at Annie's Antiques?" I asked.

"I'll go, too," she said as she loaded her books in her backpack and I unloaded mine into my locker. "I have nothing to do this afternoon."

I was planning on buying goodies for the party. How could I do that in front of her?

"Are you sure?" I asked. "You know how I can dawdle forever. I don't want you to miss doing your homework."

"I've already finished it during study hall," she said proudly.

"Then why are you taking home all your books?"

"The real question is why didn't you take any of yours?"

Becky was as good a student as she was a friend.

"I have things on my mind," I said. "I planned on doing my homework in the morning."

She shook her head, as my mother had done a thousand times.

We exited the building, got into her truck, and drove the few miles to Annie's.

Annie's Antiques was one of my favorite haunts. A Victorian-style home was turned into an antiques store, each room filled with knickknacks, furniture, and artwork.

Annie greeted me with a warm hello. She was one of the few store owners who didn't judge me by the way I was dressed, assuming I was going to vandalize or shoplift. The antiques store was also one of the few stops in Dullsville where I regularly bought merchandise.

She wore an oversized leopard-print shirt with a black faux-fur collar and black rayon pants. Two golden retrievers roamed throughout the rooms and slept by Annie's stool. "What are you looking for today?" she asked.

"Nothing in particular. Just browsing."

"I got some new things in that might interest you," she said, pointing to a nearby doorway.

I strode across the Victorian home's hardwood floors, which were weathered by all the foot traffic and furniture being moved in and out. On a small table covered with black lace fabric were items from Halloweens past.

Coveting all the goodies, I gathered as many things as I could hold, as if at any moment there could be a swarm of competitive shoppers.

"You could use a shopping cart," Becky said, helping me place the various decorations on the counter.

"Look at these!" Becky presented me with three fake tombstones. "You can put them in your room."

"Absolutely!"

I found a box of skeleton lights perfect for hanging by the gazebo.

"I'm not sure that all the bulbs work," Annie confessed when I brought them to my already rising pile of merchandise.

"It doesn't matter," I said, unfazed. "They are a must-have."

I found some lace place mats, dragon-headed candlesticks, and a ceramic raven.

"Are you having a party?" Annie asked. "You could decorate a mansion with all this stuff."

Becky gave me a skeptical stare. "Yes, what are you going to do with all these things?"

I handed Annie all the money I had in my wallet. "Saving them for a rainy day, I guess."

"It might not rain for a while," Annie said. "I hope you are able to enjoy them before then."

"I will."

Becky gave me a quizzical look as she helped carry the bags and load them into her truck.

"Need help taking them into your room?" she asked when we arrived at my house.

"That's okay," I said. "I really should do my homework, after all."

That's all I needed to say to let Becky know something was up.

"There's something you're not telling me," she said.

"You know I tell you everything—or at least everything I can share that I don't mind Matt knowing," I said, giving her a friendly dig.

"Fair enough," she said. "But I'll find out from you one way or another."

With that, Becky drove off. As I set down my goods on the driveway and unlocked my front door, I still felt a twinge of guilt. Becky had just helped me decorate a party I wasn't even inviting her to attend.

Dusk settled over Dullsville as I anxiously awaited Alexander's arrival at the cemetery.

We were going to share a private moment together before discussing our final plans for the party.

It was unusually late. I realized we might have planned to meet at the Mansion. I had finally decided to head back to the entrance when I got a text. Again, it was from an unavailable number.

I'm watching you . . .

I was sick of Trevor bothering me, and his game was about to end. I pressed the redial button, prepared to chew him out.

I heard a ringing coming from behind me but saw no one. I rose and followed the ringing until I made my way up toward the Sterling monument.

Out from the darkness emerged Alexander, a cell phone ringing in his hand.

My heart stopped. It couldn't be. Alexander had a cell phone—and had been texting me?

"It goes against everything you believe in."

He smiled a broad smile.

"It was you—all along?" I asked, still shocked.

He continued to beam.

"But you sent me messages during the day," I said, "when you were sleeping in your coffin."

"You're not the only one who gets insomnia."

The image of Alexander lying in his coffin, thinking of me and texting, melted me.

"But what made you do this?"

"I've always wanted to sit next to you in class. Buy your lunch. Watch you study. You should have all the things a normal girl gets from her boyfriend. And by going out with me . . ."

"I'm not normal, though, no matter who I go out with," I said with a laugh. "At least these Dullsvillians don't think so."

He put his arm around me. "You aren't normal to me, either. You are extraordinary."

I wrapped my arms around him.

"You should have all the good things coming to you," he continued. "All the gifts. I don't want you to ever doubt how much I care for you."

I took his free hand in mine. "But this isn't your thing. Technology. Modern conveniences."

"It's not about what's my thing," he said with a smile. "It's about yours."

I hugged Alexander with all my might.

"But I don't want you to change."

"It's not about changing—it's about growing, together," he said, like the wise soul that he was. "I wanted to let you know—that I am with you. Always. Forever. We don't have to be separated by the sun, school, or even the night. Now I'm just a click away."

I was deeply moved by Alexander's present to me and rewarded my vampire boyfriend with mortal kisses.

15

Party at the Mansion

I spent the following day alone, toiling around in the Mansion's backyard while Alexander and Sebastian slept in their respective tombs. No one would be able to help me set up for the party. That's what I got for wanting to date a vampire.

I hung the skeleton lights from the wrought-iron fence and put place mats on a coffin-lid table. I lined the crumbling walkway with votives and floor-length candelabras. The fake tombstones poked out from the dead grass. Sebastian had hooked up his sound system in the gazebo, and I decorated it with plastic bats and blinking skulls.

By the time Alexander and Sebastian awoke, I was beat. The pair was wide-eyed and freshly groomed when they found me crashed out on a sofa in the parlor room.

Alexander gently petted my hair and awakened me from my catnap.

The best sight in the world was Alexander. Even blurry, he was smoldering. His deep, dark hair melted over his ears, and his smile was heavenly.

"You've really outdone yourself," he said. "The back-yard looks great!"

"What time is it?" I perked up in a hurry.

"They should be here soon," he said.

"I'm not even dressed!" I exclaimed. "And I feel like I just got out of gym class."

I leaped up from the sofa and dashed to the upstairs bathroom.

I only had twenty minutes to clean up. I washed, dried, primped, powdered. It was something I was used to, as I normally overslept and had to get ready for school in record time.

Also, I was extra speedy because I was anxious for our party to begin, eager to see Onyx and Scarlet, and for Sebastian to fall in love with one of them so my relationship with Becky would return to normal.

When I finished my fifteen-minute makeover, I descended the outside backstairs as if I were a contestant in a beauty pageant. Only, instead of stilettos, hose, and a white ball gown, I was in rubber lace-up boots, fishnets, and a black slip dress. I spun around in my outfit.

"Boy—you look hot!" Alexander said. He was setting up the fire pit.

"Make that double hot!" Sebastian concurred.

Sebastian was tinkering with the sound system, making sure his favorite hits were loaded onto his iPod. The three of us talked for a while, but our monsterfest wasn't going as planned. There was no sign of Onyx and Scarlet.

Alexander stoked the fire. Sebastian fixed some of the skeleton lights, and I adjusted my suffocating boots.

"It's been nightfall for over an hour," I finally commented, glancing at my watch. "Where are they?"

"Maybe they got lost," Alexander said. "Did you give them directions?"

"Several times."

"Then I bet something else came up," Sebastian lamented.

"I know these girls," I said defiantly. "If they said they'd be here—"

"It's okay, Raven," Sebastian said. "It's really the nicest thing anyone has ever done for me. But we don't have to wait all night. Besides, this is as good a time as any to tell you that I'll be leaving tomorrow."

"What?" I asked.

Even Alexander was surprised by his comment. "We were having a blast."

"I know . . . but I've worn out my welcome here." ·

"No, you haven't," I told him. I'd gotten used to Sebastian's presence, and I knew it was good for Alexander to have the company.

"Why don't we go inside," he suggested. "We can have a little band session to take it off my mind. I think you're on your way to being a lead singer."

"We can't give up on our party yet," I tried.

Even Alexander was getting a bit fidgety. "We haven't

eaten yet and I'm feeling hungry. We'll have Jameson make us some drinks."

"But you have a bottle out here," I told them.

"We'll save it for something special," Alexander said.

"Fine." My first party, and it was a disaster.

They headed inside. I remained at the table and sulked for a few moments until I heard a car in the distance. I took off around the side of the grassy Mansion lawn, doing my best to avoid uneven patches of soil. When I reached the driveway, I saw two headlights shining on the street. The streetlamp illuminated a car. When I got closer I noticed a bright white Beetle, the headlights highlighted with black paint, the hood with a dark circle, and vertical white stripes adorning the bumper. It looked like a giant human skull.

"They're here!" I exclaimed. "They're here."

I raced down the long driveway as if I were competing for a gold medal.

When I reached the Mansion's gate, exiting the cryptic car were two amazingly stellar party girls—Scarlet and Onyx.

Scarlet wore her curly red hair long with a black bow; she had on a cream-colored velvet dress, black lace gloves, and stilettos. Onyx, with her jet black, blade-straight hair, wore a corset top, knee-length skirt, ripped stockings, and wicked witchy boots.

We all screamed like children, and they engulfed me in a tight embrace.

"We thought we'd never see you again," Scarlet said.

"I thought so, too," I said.

"When we saw your message, we knew we had to come," Onyx said. "No matter what."

"I love your car!" I proclaimed. I could only dream of driving that up to my house in the burbs. I thought I was lucky to have a black bike.

"I just got it. Isn't it ghoulish?" Scarlet grinned.

The two girls linked arms with me and we ascended the steep and winding drive. It was as if we were miniature dolls in comparison to the stately Mansion that loomed above us.

"Is this where you live?" Onyx asked, aghast.

"No, my boyfriend does," I replied.

"Are his parents out for the weekend?" Scarlet wondered, assessing the situation.

"Well—for a while longer," I said. "They live in Romania."

"He lives here by himself?" Onyx asked. "How lonely."

"He has a butler."

"You go, girl!" Scarlet said.

"He must be a millionaire," Onyx stated.

"Almost," I said.

"Is he . . . a V?" Onyx asked.

"A what?" I wondered aloud.

"A Coffin Club member," Scarlet whispered. "You know—one of us . . ."

"Oh . . . a V." I nodded proudly. "And more important, so is his friend."

"He has a friend?" Scarlet hinted.

"Yes, and he's single and very hot," I replied.

"Love it!" the two girls shrieked.

"We never see that Phoenix guy anymore," Scarlet said. "We thought maybe you'd have hooked up with him."

"Really?" I asked. "Well . . . I haven't either. But I think you'll like Alexander, too."

"Judging from that Mansion? I like him already," Scarlet declared.

Alexander didn't realize that the girls had arrived. The backyard was empty of male vampires. I was slightly miffed at the pair for giving up so easily.

"Where is everyone?" Scarlet said.

"They went inside."

I felt awful. Should I leave my guests alone? Or take them inside? I had never hosted a party before and wasn't sure of the etiquette. I knew my mother would know exactly what to do, so I did my best impression of her.

"Why don't you two wait here while I get you something to drink," I asked.

"No—stay with us," Onyx said, grasping my wrist. "We traveled all this way to see you, so we're not letting you out of our sight."

"Yes," Scarlet said. "This way we can have some girl time."

I wanted the girls to feel the full effects of our haunting happening, but without Alexander and Sebastian it wasn't happening at all.

Maybe Alexander would get worried and come find me.

We sat at the tomb-shaped table. A Romanian bottle

was chilling on ice, and the twinkling candelabra was still dripping hot wax.

"So how's the Coffin Club?" I asked. "I miss it."

"It's the best," Onyx said.

"There isn't anywhere we've found that's like it," Scarlet added. "And since Phoenix usurped Jagger's authority and made the club about us and not him, it's been running smoothly. But we haven't seen Phoenix at all. It's quite odd."

"We thought you might have seen him," Onyx began, "since you got on so well with him."

"I haven't seen anybody."

"Not even Jagger?" Onyx asked.

"No—and for that I'm grateful."

"Really? I think he's kind of hot," Onyx confessed.

Scarlet and I were surprised by her admission of admiration for the alluring, but menacing, vampire.

"I mean in a lonely sort of way," Onyx continued. "I think he might just be misunderstood. . . ."

"So . . . ," Scarlet said. "You're dating a vampire. Then you'll become a vampire, too!" Scarlet was beside herself with glee.

"Uh . . . we're waiting for the right time," I answered.

"But don't you want to be like us?" Scarlet asked.

"Of course," I replied. "It's been my life's dream."

"Then what are you waiting for—"

"It's a big decision," Onyx defended. "I don't know that I'd turn someone. It is a lot of responsibility."

"I would!" Scarlet said. "It's in our blood."

"To change someone's life forever?" Onxy proposed. "We were born into this. We didn't have a choice. And for Raven, it would be changing everything about her life as she knows it. It is something that should be thought through really carefully. Not so casual or in the moment," Onyx argued, reassuring me. "It's okay, Raven, to take your time."

"There is nothing wrong with being a vampire," Scarlet said.

"I didn't say there was," Onyx retorted. "But would you want to be mortal—if you found your true love?"

Scarlet thought for a moment. "I guess you're right. It is a big decision."

I smiled in agreement. It was hard—these two girls took for granted a lifestyle I wanted so badly. They weren't becoming vampires because of someone they loved or something they wanted to be—they were vampires because they were born vampires.

It was then I remembered why I'd invited them.

"Speaking of true love . . . ," I began. "I've got a really great guy I want you to meet."

"Yes, tell us about Alexander's friend," Onxy said.

"He's really hot," I repeated. "And he's looking for someone special."

"We're special," Scarlet said.

"Exactly! That was what I was thinking." I scooted close. "He was enamored with my best friend," I confided. "Only, she's mortal and has a boyfriend. And I don't want anyone in this town being bitten before me," I joked.

"Yes, that wouldn't be fair," Onyx said.

"I'd die if some cheerleader showed up to a game with fangs," I told them.

"That would be wrong on so many levels!" Scarlet snorted.

"She wouldn't be deserving," Onyx said. "Not like you."

"So I thought it would be wonderful if he could meet a nice vampire girl," I went on. "And Dullsville is short on those."

"So where is this Prince Charming?" Scarlet asked.

The faint sound of a guitar wailing screeched from the Mansion.

"Is that your boyfriend playing?" Scarlet asked tentatively.

"No—that's his friend."

"I hope he kisses better than he plays," she teased.

The three of us laughed.

A figure was standing by the window. I knew Alexander would eventually wonder where I'd gone.

Within a moment, Alexander and Sebastian were hanging out on the back steps.

Both girls' mouths dropped when they saw the handsome pair.

"Which is the available one?" Onyx asked softly.

"I don't care—they are both gorgeous," Scarlet declared. "Raven—you don't mind sharing, do you?" she teased.

"Onyx and Scarlet, this is my boyfriend, Alexander."

"Wow—you are so lucky!" Scarlet whispered to me.

"We should have been hanging out here instead of at the Coffin Club."

Alexander blushed and shook both of their hands.

Sebastian cleared his throat. He was frustrated he wasn't getting any attention.

"And this is Sebastian," I said. As if on cue, both girls held their hands out to him. He took each one and tenderly kissed them. Each girl giggled.

"I hope that's just a prelude of what's to come," Scarlet said.

The girls broke their gaze with Sebastian and he gave Alexander the thumbs-up sign.

"Would you like something to drink?" I asked.

"Uh. Sure. I guess I'll have a soda."

"No, we have the real thing," Sebastian said, pointing to the bottle on the table.

"Transylvania 1972," Alexander said as Jameson came outside to assist us.

"I heard that was a good year," Sebastian said.

"Why don't you sit here," I encouraged Sebastian, deliberately placing him between the two girls.

Alexander stuck a corkscrew in the bottle and turned it slowly. He pried the cork and it easily slipped out.

Jameson began filling the goblets.

"It's rare to find something authentic—outside the Coffin Club," Scarlet said. "In a bottle, anyway."

We all laughed.

"Well, you are in rare company," Sebastian flirted.

As Jameson continued to fill the goblets, Alexander

poured me a soda and then himself one.

"You can have some," I said. "Don't miss this on account of me."

But Alexander politely refused.

Sebastian held the goblet to his nose and took a deep breath in.

"Um . . . perfect," Sebastian said. "I think it's a mixture of A positive and AB negative."

"Wow—you are quite the connoisseur," Onyx praised. "I can never tell."

"Here's to us." Sebastian raised his glass and we all clinked ours together.

I watched as the three vampires put the blood-filled goblets to their lips and sipped as if they were consuming a rare vintage wine.

"This is delicious," Scarlet said. "Very smooth."

"We are just happy you joined us," Alexander said. "We know you came a long way."

"It was worth it," Scarlet said.

"Very smooth," Onyx added. "Yet sweet. Just like you," she said, her eyes locking with Sebastian's. Surprised by her remark, she began to giggle and spilled a bit of her drink.

I had to remind myself that some Romanian's hemoglobin, not fermented grapes, had just dripped on my friend.

"She can't hold her blood," Scarlet playfully scolded. "I tell her that all the time."

"I guess I drank it too fast," Onyx said.

Red liquid dripped down her neck and began leaking toward the lace border of her neckline.

"Here, let me," Sebastian said, wiping the spillage with his napkin.

There was a moment between Onyx and Sebastian. He was doting on her as he had Becky. Our plan was already working. I gave Alexander a quick wink.

Scarlet sensed competition. And though the two girls were best friends, it was obvious Scarlet didn't want to be the one without a vampire. She leaned her elbow onto Sebastian's shoulder, her bracelets dangling next to his goatee.

She tapped her fingers against his brown and blond dreadlocks as if they were batting eyelashes, then brushed her plum-colored fingernails along his neck.

"No recent marks . . . ," she noted.

"Interesting," Onyx said, almost scorned.

"And you?" Sebastian asked Scarlet.

"It isn't polite to ask a girl, is it?" she asked coquettishly.

"Well, I just thought."

Scarlet displayed her wrist. Two purple marks were embedded on her slight, chalk white arm.

"But it didn't really mean anything," she confessed. "He wasn't nearly as handsome as you."

"Or as clever," Onyx added.

The girls were intoxicated by Sebastian's charm, and he was relishing the attention.

I figured this was mine and Alexander's cue to leave the three single vampires alone.

"Alexander, I think we left a few snacks in the house," I said.

"Oh yeah," my boyfriend agreed, taking my hint. "I'll help you."

But before we could rise, Scarlet stopped us. "Where is everyone else?"

"Oh . . . they'll be coming later," Sebastian said.

"Yeah. We just wanted it to be us for a little while," I added.

"Then sit down and enjoy yourselves," Scarlet insisted.

Alexander and I returned to our seats. I guess the girls expected a Mansion-size party. I couldn't break the news to them that they were the guest list.

"How about we crank up the tunes," Sebastian suggested.

"Yes, we love to dance," Scarlet said.

Sebastian turned up the music and the five of us rocked as hard as we could.

"It looks like you're having a great time," I said to Sebastian as I danced next to him.

"I am."

"Do you think you'd like to ask one of them out?"

"I guess." But Sebastian's voice wasn't confident. Even though he was having a blast, I sensed Sebastian was still carrying a torch for Becky.

The music's volume suddenly lowered. We stopped to discover Jameson standing by the sound system.

"Complaints from the neighbors?" Alexander asked, concerned.

"Alexander," Jameson announced, "you have some guests."

"Guests?" I asked.

Alexander was just as confused.

"I'll only be a moment," he said, excusing himself.

"I guess they're here," Scarlet said. "We'll chat later."

I was curious what guests were arriving. Since Onyx, Scarlet, and Sebastian were engaged in conversation, I, too, excused myself.

I sped through the kitchen, down the long, haunting hallway, and found Alexander at the front door. I couldn't tell whom he was talking to, so I sneaked up close and peered out.

I spotted Becky's truck in the driveway.

What was she doing here? Was she in trouble?

It was then I noticed Trevor's Camaro parked behind the truck.

I wedged myself between the entranceway and Alexander to find Matt fuming at the foot of the stoop.

"What's going on?" I asked. "Are you all right?"

Matt, normally upbeat and smiling, was brandishing a frown. Behind him was Trevor and a team of soccer snobs.

"What are they doing here?" I asked Alexander.

Matt glared at me coldly.

"It's okay," Alexander said to me.

"Where's Becky?" I asked. "Is she all right?"

"I thought you were my friend, Alexander," Matt said sternly.

Alexander didn't move. "I am," he said calmly. "What's this all about, Matt?"

"Your houseguest."

"He's out back."

"Well, he better stay there."

"Is something wrong?" Alexander asked.

"You bet. Your best friend has been hitting on my girlfriend," Matt challenged.

Alexander shook his head. His best friend had gotten him into a mess. "That's just Sebastian's way. He didn't mean any harm."

"Did you know that after Sebastian met Becky at Hatsy's he texted her all night?" Matt asked.

"Not at the time. I'm not with him every minute."

"Sebastian sent the flowers to Becky. Not Raven. Did you know that?"

"No—or I would have stopped him."

"But you did find out."

"Yes."

"So were you going to tell me?"

"There wasn't a need to. We had it resolved."

"Really? Did you know he had the nerve to show up at her house?"

"He did?" Alexander said. "I thought he bumped into her in town."

"And all the time you both were laughing and encouraging him," Matt said, annoyed.

"Now, take it easy. I never laughed, and I most certainly didn't encourage him. It was just the opposite."

Now I was mad. It was one thing to accuse me, and now Sebastian, of causing trouble, but quite another to accuse

Alexander. "You have it wrong, Matt. Alexander—"

"It's okay, Raven," Alexander said, trying to calm me down. "I understand you might be mad, Matt. But it's not as bad as it sounds."

"And to think I included him at Hooligans."

"You are misunderstanding what happened."

"Am I?"

Matt stepped forward.

I was ready to pounce on anyone who charged at Alexander—though he was quite capable of defending himself.

Alexander held out his arm. "It's okay."

"Now you're having a party," Matt said. Then he fixed on me. "And Raven—you don't invite your best friend?"

Trevor stood behind Matt, arms folded, smiling gleefully.

"What's he doing here?" I charged. "I thought you weren't his shadow anymore."

"He's the one who told me," Matt said. "Seems Trevor is a good friend after all."

The soccer snobs surrounded Alexander. I rushed in, but Alexander held me at bay.

"I don't think you know who you are dealing with here," I said to the gang of athletes.

Alexander appeared concerned for Matt's situation, but he wasn't worried about the threat from the others. He was confident in his own power, and I knew he wouldn't use it unless it was to defend me.

"Is Becky with Sebastian?" Alexander asked.

"No—she's with me," Matt said.

"Then isn't that your answer?" Alexander assured Matt. "After all the texts, the flowers, and the visits, she's still with you."

Matt's anger changed to relief. He even broke a smile.

Sebastian suddenly appeared beside us. "What's going on?"

When he saw Matt, he knew he must have found out about his feelings for Becky.

"I'm the one you have a beef with," Sebastian said. "This isn't about Alexander."

"I know that now," Matt said.

"Let's talk calmly," Sebastian urged.

"I know how you feel about Becky—but I'm the one who loves her," Matt suddenly proclaimed.

Becky hopped out of the truck. She raced to Matt and clutched him around the waist. He'd declared his love for her in front of everyone. She gazed up at me with an almost thankful smile.

I was surprised by Matt's sudden passion and proud that he was standing up for Becky. However, I didn't want this conflict to continue.

"And just so you know," Sebastian defended, "Alexander ordered me to leave the Mansion."

"He did?" Matt asked.

"But I was the one who wanted to stay in town. Raven and Alexander went out of their way to arrange a party for me—to find my own Becky. So they really are better friends to you than you might think."

Matt was speechless.

"Yeah—so you might have Becky," Sebastian began, "but I have Raven and Alexander."

Matt was stunned. "I feel awful," he said.

"I do, too," Becky added.

Matt glared at Trevor. "You started this, didn't you? Just like always."

But Trevor's attention was on a few cars that had pulled up to the Mansion's gate.

Within a few minutes, vehicles began to line the street.

Students came up the driveway and the lawn, decked out in their Saturday-night best and carrying bags of beverages.

"What's going on?" I asked.

"You know how news travels in this town," Trevor said. "Everyone likes a party. Not just you guys."

"Where's the coffin guy?" a Pradabee asked.

"Is that him?" another asked, pointing to Alexander. "He's gorgeous!"

"I wonder if he has a dungeon," the Pradabee commented. "Or a secret room. I wouldn't mind if he locked me up in one." The pair laughed and followed the others to the backyard.

"What are we going to do?" I asked frantically. "Call the police?"

"No—it's fine." Alexander beamed.

Alexander surveyed his uninvited guests and their festive mood.

"Well, we don't have enough drinks," I said. "I mean, the non-Romanian kind."

"Doesn't seem to matter. Looks like they are bringing their own," Alexander commented.

Sebastian lit up. "Now, this is a real party. This is what we're missing by being homeschooled. Look at these girls. They're all hot!"

We arrived in the backyard to a full-fledged happening. The backyard began to fill up with every teen in town.

"Here's some liquor," a soccer snob said, holding the unfinished Transylvania 1972.

He lifted it to his lips and leaned back to take a huge swig.

"No—" I yanked it out of his hands. "That's an import!" I chastised. I grabbed the goblets and carried them into the house like a seasoned waitress.

As I exited, I met an anxious Jameson in the doorway, examining the expanding party.

"Miss Raven, what has happened?"

"We had a few party crashers."

"A few? More like a hundred. I must go to the basement. I know we have more stock."

"Not the cellar, Jameson," I said. "It's not that kind of party."

"Of course, I meant in the downstairs pantry." Jameson fretted. "Oh, I wish I had time to prepare!"

I'd watched plenty of movies. Couples using pieces of furniture and empty bedrooms for makeout sessions while others used the furniture as coasters. I didn't want the Mansion trashed and, more important, Alexander's and Sebastian's identity revealed. "Don't let anyone in the house," I told Jameson before he started off. "If they find Sebastian's bed . . ."

"I understand, Miss Raven."

Just then two girls came up to the door.

"Which way to the bathroom?" one asked.

"That way," I said, pointing to the street. "There is one at the gas station. Or, better yet, I bet there's a golden-scated one at your home. . . ."

The girls glowered at me and returned to their boyfriends.

"I'll stand watch as soon as I get back," he said nervously. Jameson wasn't the only one upset. I returned to find my party—like my life—out of control.

Couples were mashing. Some were hanging out by the fire pit. Others were dancing.

I spotted Onyx and Scarlet hovering on either side of Trevor. The girls were fawning over his beefy physique.

Where was Sebastian? The girls were supposed to be drooling over him. But none of the vampires seemed interested in the others at this point.

I stormed through the crowd and toward the girls. Scarlet pretended to arm-wrestle with Trevor and then turned his wrist to examine it.

I saw Scarlet's fang catch the light of the fire pit. Onyx's onyx tattooed fang sparkled when she grinned.

Trevor was in heaven. But if Onyx and Scarlet had their way, he might be somewhere else.

Scarlet lifted his wrist to her mouth.

"Scarlet!" I called. "Onyx."

"Not so fast," Trevor warned, holding Onyx by the waist. "They are doing just fine. You aren't the only one interested in threesomes."

"First of all, I'm not. And second of all, this isn't that kind of party."

"Is jealousy the only emotion you feel?" Trevor charged. "Even in front of Monster Boy?" he said. "But it appears he's already busy," he said, gesturing to a few girls who were talking to Alexander. "But don't worry. You can join in with us. . . . I won't tell."

I wasn't pleased that my schoolmates were fawning over my boyfriend, but I had more urgent matters to attend to.

"Save it for school."

I wrangled the girls away from Trevor and whispered in Onyx's ear. "He's not a *V*."

"Not a *V*?" He had overheard me. "What does that mean? *Virgin?*"

"Oh, really?" Onyx said softly.

They were shocked.

"Funny, we both sensed he was," Scarlet whispered. "It's not the first time we've made a mistake," she said, alluding to me.

"Remember why I invited you guys—for Sebastian," I urged.

But Scarlet wasn't walking away. She was charmed by Trevor and continued to hold on to his hand.

"You can have Sebastian," she said in a low voice to Onyx.

"She can't like Trevor," I said. "That's not an option. Remember what we discussed," I warned through gritted teeth. "No one gets—"

"Don't worry, Raven. She's just having fun," Onyx said, stopping me. "And I plan to do the same." Onyx flipped back her jet black locks and disappeared into the crowd.

This party was getting out of hand. Vampires mixing with unsuspecting mortals. I had to make sure no one was bitten—especially Trevor Mitchell.

I looked to Alexander and Sebastian for help. Sebastian was now talking to the girls who were interested in Alexander, and Alexander was entranced by his rocking party.

I turned to go back to Trevor and I bumped into Becky.

"I'm so sorry, Raven," she said. "Can you forgive me?"

"Uh, yes—but I have something else I have to deal with right now."

"Please—listen," Becky pleaded. "You're the one who always talks about being in trouble, but I'm the one who keeps getting you there. You are my best friend. Now and always—and I don't want anything to get in the way of that."

"I hated not telling you about the party," I said. "I did feel like a sneak. But I had to protect you."

"I totally understand. You and Alexander are so kind to Sebastian—and to me. And look what we've done. We brought Trevor and the entire school to the Mansion." Becky sat on a bench lined with plastic skeletons. "I'm so ashamed."

"It's okay, Becky." I gave her a hug. "Alexander's having the time of his life. Babes dancing in his backyard. Jocks hanging out. It's an image I never imagined. It's a blessing, really. He's so isolated being homeschooled, and now he's more popular than Trevor."

Becky managed a small grimace. "You don't hate me?"

"Of course I don't hate you. You'd have to do a lot worse than bringing Trevor to the Mansion for me to not like you. But speaking of Trevor—I have a major issue to address. Can you help me?"

"Of course."

Just as I began pushing past the crowd to separate an embracing Trevor and Scarlet, all heads turned toward the back stairs.

I saw a sight I thought I'd never see. I was completely unprepared.

Descending down the Mansion's back stairs as if a soft halo of light were around her was a gothic fairy girl with candy-pink-colored hair perfectly woven into two braids and wrapped in Wednesday Addams–style black bows, wearing an offbeat Alice in Wonderland dress with black-and-white tights and pink combat boots.

She was as beautiful as she was cute, as fragile as she was confident. Her frame was that of a whimsical angel with the wings of a devil. And everyone at the party was spellbound.

It was Luna Maxwell.

I hated how beautiful she was. She had perfectly porcelain skin, and her glossy pink lips sparkled like tiny stars.
Her presence lit up the crowd. She drew everyone's attention like a starlet.

The crowd was hypnotized. Sebastian was mesmerized.
For a moment, even Alexander was transfixed.

And looming right behind her was her twin brother—
Jagger, Alexander's former nemesis—sporting familiar
bleached-white hair with bloodred ends, a freakishly fright-
ening Joker T-shirt, and red Doc Martens.

Our party had officially spun out of this world.

How was I going to hold all these vampires at bay from
mixing with the mortal students of Dullsville? How were
we going to keep their Underworldly identity a secret? And
if their cover was blown, how was I going to keep Alexander from having to leave Dullsville?

My blood boiled and my flesh flushed. I felt dizzy and
queasy. The voices and music became muddled, and everyone suddenly seemed very far away.

I was sure I was falling.

Then the world went black.

16

Spin the Bloody Bottle

I opened my eyes to find myself lying flat on the grass. Alexander was kneeling beside me. A large circle of familiar faces—Becky, Matt, Onyx, Sebastian, Scarlet, Trevor, Jagger, and Luna—were staring down at me. The stars shimmered and a full moon hovered above them.

It had to be a dream.

I closed my eyes again.

"Let's give her some air," I heard a girl's voice say.

"Did you drink too much?" another asked.

"Did she take something?"

"Did she OD?" someone else said.

My mouth was dry. I couldn't form a word in my defense.

"I'll take her to a doctor," Alexander said, alarmed.

"Here, drink this," Becky said, handing me a soda. Alexander helped me sit up, and I gulped down the bubbly liquid as if I hadn't drunk for days.

Scarlet held a bag of ice on my head.

"Did you eat something odd?" Becky asked like a ponytailed Florence Nightingale.

"No—I haven't eaten anything," I replied, weakened.

The crowd of well-wishers stopped fussing.

"What?" Alexander asked. "You haven't eaten?"

"I didn't have time. I was decorating for the party all day."

"Not even breakfast?" Scarlet asked.

"No."

"Then no wonder you fainted," Becky said.

Alexander signaled to Sebastian, who took off for the Mansion.

My boyfriend swept me up in his arms and carried me to the table. He gently let me down in a wrought-iron chair and held my hand while I drank my soda. A few moments later, Jameson pushed a small cart through the crowd of partygoers. The scent of marinated steak was intoxicating to the mortals and euphoric to the vampires.

A thick, juicy steak was placed before me. All the vampires, including Alexander, almost salivated.

"I'll do that," Scarlet said as I began to cut into the bloody steak.

"It's for Raven," Alexander said gently.

The vampires watched with envy as I tore into my

meal. As I wolfed down the steak and began to regain my strength, Alexander began to address the next issue we had on our hands—bloodsucking party crashers.

The candelabras lit Jagger's menacing ice-green-and-blue eyes. His sister stood behind him, basking in the glow of stares from the male partyers.

"I don't remember inviting—" Alexander said.

"Some girls have looser lips than others," Jagger said.

Onyx appeared ashamed.

"Perhaps it's time we mingle," Scarlet said. She led Onyx into the crowd.

"We didn't think you'd mind," Jagger said to Alexander. "Now that we are friends."

Alexander was skeptical. Though their feud had ended when Alexander returned Jagger's weakened brother, Valentine, to him, Alexander wasn't expecting his longtime nemesis to instantly replace Sebastian.

"Friends?" Alexander said.

"Yes," Jagger said. "One can never have too many, right?"

"I suppose you are right, but—"

"There really is safety in numbers," Jagger urged. "Besides, we have so much in common: Romania, vampires, and Raven."

"Raven?" Alexander asked suspiciously.

"I saw a lot of her recently," Jagger proclaimed, referring to my attendance at the Coffin Club. "She fit right in."

"I heard," Alexander said.

"No one knew she was any different. Did she tell you?"

"She didn't have to."

"I was hoping to see her there again," Jagger continued. "It seemed she got on as well as any of the members there."

"She is planning on being here," Alexander said.

"I was hoping you'd come back," Jagger said to me. "But since you didn't, this way we've come to you."

"How sweet," I retorted.

"I think we'll be fast friends, Alexander," Jagger said. "It's something I've always wanted. There is so much we can learn from each other." Jagger gestured to the party. "There is safety in numbers. We could use more members and, with your help, perhaps start a club here."

"Out of the question!" Alexander said.

"Nothing you have to decide now, my friend," Jagger said calmly. "But imagine . . . If all these mortals were just like us, then think of what could be—what we could do. A town in which you don't have to hide out in a Mansion, all alone."

"I think it's time you leave," Alexander demanded.

"But we just got here," Jagger said. "You're right. I'm getting ahead of myself. I'm just a visionary, that's all. Nothing you need to commit to this minute. Besides," Jagger continued, "we came to party. And Luna was very eager to see Raven."

"So how have you been, Raven?" she asked, über-polite. "Besides lying flat on your back," she whispered in my ear.

Luna was still bitter toward me for fooling her into believing I was a vampire. And even more so because Alexander had jilted her at the covenant ceremony back in Romania and he had found happiness with me.

However, seeing Luna standing here today, glowing like an angel, I couldn't imagine him ever leaving her.

"Alexander," Luna said in a soft, sexy voice. "It's great to see you." She showed off her dress for him. A group of jocks ogled her as she twirled around. "It's amazing how much a person can change in just a short time, isn't it? I'm sorry for you that things in your life have remained the same."

Alexander wasn't pleased with her taunting.

"Yes, doesn't my sister look great?" Jagger said. "This lifestyle suits her. She's been dying for it since she was born."

"I'm glad you are so happy," Alexander said. "That's all I ever wanted for you." He turned back to the party.

Luna took Alexander's comment as a slap in the face instead of a heartfelt sentiment. She couldn't mask her scorn and turned her venom on me.

"I see you've managed to fool some other girls, too," she said, referring to Onyx and Scarlet.

"They like me for who I am," I said.

"But do you like yourself as you are? Or, at the end of the day, do you really wish you were more like me?"

Luna was right. She had the one thing I didn't have—she was a vampire.

"I have everything you've always wanted," she bragged.

"Except Alexander," I snapped back.

"Well, when you can be here for an eternity, everything is possible. I just need time."

I wasn't happy with her insinuation.

"When he sees my potential. Perhaps what he is missing from a relationship with you . . . Who knows what he might do?"

With that, she and Jagger joined the other partygoers.

"Alexander," I said, getting his attention, "Luna isn't over you. She still can't be trusted."

"Her bark is worse than her bite."

"I'm serious. She's still in love with—"

"Hey," Sebastian said, suddenly by our side. "This party is killer!"

"You think so?" I asked.

"It's not what I planned. *I'm* even amazed." Alexander beamed.

"This mansion is going to be party central," said Sebastian. "The girls think you are a rock star, and I don't mind taking your leftovers."

I glared at Sebastian.

"I mean, taking them off your hands so you can be alone with Raven."

A band of jocks bumped into the tomb-shaped table, knocking it over. Alexander rushed to help steady it.

"There is no reason you need to be cruising this crowd," I told Sebastian. "There are two perfect and single girls—that were just meant for you," I said as the ultimate matchmaker. "Onyx or Scarlet."

"I know, Raven. They are beautiful, but there aren't any sparks."

"What do you mean? You just met them. And now you are totally ignoring them. You need to spend more time with them."

"It's just something I feel—or rather don't feel. And by the way it looks, they don't seem to be bothered."

Trevor was talking to Jagger, and Onyx and Scarlet were by their sides.

"Well, maybe I'm not meant to be in love," he said. "Maybe I'm supposed to just have fun. And is that so bad?"

I was a major failure at matchmaking.

"This was not supposed to happen!" I said. "None of this was supposed to happen!"

I ditched Sebastian and was heading toward Alexander when Becky jumped in front of me.

"Where have you been?" she asked.

"This night has gone all wrong," I said frantically.

"No it hasn't. Look! Everyone is enjoying themselves. You might be having the best party Dullsville's ever seen."

"Sebastian was supposed to like Scarlet or Onyx and he doesn't like either," I rambled, "and to top it off, Scarlet seems to be struck by Trevor—gag me—and Onyx is smitten by Jagger."

"It's nice that they came to town for your party."

"Jagger and Luna weren't invited. Remember? You weren't even invited."

Becky laughed. "Raven, you've brought the whole town together—even a neighboring one."

"But I didn't want to. Even Jameson is freaking out." He was standing guard outside the kitchen door. "I have to do something. I know . . ." I took out my phone. "I'll call the police. A noise complaint and a few squad cars are enough to drive everyone back to their sprawling estates."

Becky stopped me. "Raven—then Alexander's party will be a bomb. Look at him." Alexander was joking with the group of jocks as they replaced the items on the table. He was as content and happy as he'd been when he was out with Sebastian and me. "Wouldn't you rather the party be a hit than have your boyfriend stuck in his attic room forever alone?"

I weighed my friend's thoughts heavily.

"Then what should I do?" I finally asked.

"How about have some fun—like everyone else? Why should you be the only one moping?"

Becky didn't understand the severity of the situation. And it wasn't something I could delicately break to her over the sounds of pounding music. However, it was Alexander's mansion, and if Alexander was having a blast, then it wasn't my place to break up the party.

Alexander was now hanging out by the fire pit with Matt, Sebastian, and several soccer snobs. I was approaching him when I overheard a few cheerleaders talking to him.

"Are you the painter in the article?" one asked.

"Uh . . . yes."

"I like to model," another told him.

"Do you do nude portraits?" the first one asked.

The girls all laughed.

I was steaming! My blood began to boil and my whole body raged.

"There is only one model I use," Alexander said. "And her name is—"

"Raven," they said in unison.

"Yes," he said.

A warm feeling flooded me.

"Perhaps you should get to know her," he said. "She's a great girl."

The girls all turned their noses at him and walked away. I snuck up behind my boyfriend and gave him a huge embrace.

"There you are," he said. "I was just talking about you."

"You have groupies," I said. "Sebastian was right."

"No I don't," he said humbly.

He drew me close and kissed me by the open flames.

"I never dreamed we'd have a hit on our hands," I said.

"I never did, either," he said.

Jagger and Onyx and Luna joined us by the fire pit.

"Jagger Maxwell," Sebastian said, a drink in his hand. "It's been a while since I've seen you. This is the last place I'd imagine bumping into you."

Jagger moved in close, out of earshot of the soccer snobs and Matt.

"Alexander and I have to make up for lost time. I thought now was as good a time as any to begin our new friendship."

"Alexander is really picky about who he hangs out with," Sebastian said protectively.

"I'm sure he is."

"Rumor is you haven't returned to Romania," Sebastian said.

"I started a club a few towns over. I've been talking to Alexander about possibly starting one here."

"This town could really use a club," Sebastian said.

Jagger's blue-and-green eyes lit up. "Then you might be the one to help me."

"I love clubs. And you're right—this town could be a perfect place to open one."

"You don't know what he's really talking about," Alexander warned.

"Perhaps we can go into business together," Jagger said to Sebastian.

"Maybe . . ."

Luna yawned and appeared bored.

"Luna," Jagger said, seizing the opportunity. "I want you to meet Alexander's best friend."

"Alexander's best friend?" she asked, perking up. "I don't believe we've met."

"No, I think I'd remember," Sebastian said, tongue-tied.

"She grew up on a different time schedule than we did. But now we are all finally the same," Jagger said. "Luna, Sebastian might be interested in starting a Coffin Club here."

"No he's not," Alexander said. "He doesn't know what you are talking about."

Sebastian was lost in Luna's spell, even though she was somewhat intimidating.

"Any friend of Alexander's is a friend of mine, right, Alexander?" Luna flirted.

"Let's hope so," Sebastian said.

"Suddenly this party doesn't seem so insipid after all," she commented.

I tried to block Sebastian from Luna. "I think Jameson needs our help in the kitchen."

"Jameson can find someone else," Luna said, gazing at Sebastian. "It's a party, the night is young, and I'm out for blood. . . . Would you like to dance, Sebastian?" Luna asked.

"Are you kidding?" Sebastian looked as if he would have breathed in garlic if Luna had asked him.

"So tell me what it was like growing up with Alexander," Luna said, leading him to the dance floor.

Jagger smiled a mischievous smile. "Onyx, would you like to dance?"

Onyx acted as if she'd just been struck by Cupid's bow. "Of course," she said, and followed Jagger.

"Alexander—what do we do?"

"How about we dance, too?"

When we arrived on the dance floor, Alexander and I kept a watchful eye on the others. But after a few songs, we got distracted by our own connection.

"This was the reason to have a party," Alexander said, kissing me. "For us."

I was so lost in his eyes. I'd gotten so sidetracked that I wasn't allowing myself to enjoy the very thing I'd been dreaming about all my life: Alexander Sterling.

"I still want to be like you," I said. "I want to be with you. Forever."

Alexander pulled me into him and laid a dizzy-making kiss on my lips—so passionate and tender, my knees shook.

Luna bore a gaze that blazed through us.

Becky and Matt applauded, and we got a few whistles.

Alexander and I embraced, and Luna left the dance floor.

"How about a slow one?" Matt suggested. He fiddled with the sound system until he found a song he liked.

The four of us danced, joined by Dullsvillian student couples.

When the song was over, I was jolted out of our romantic entanglement.

The Pradabees were with the other Pradabees, and the soccer snobs were mixing it up with the cheerleaders. Trevor was flirting with Scarlet, and Onyx was hanging next to Jagger.

"Where's Sebastian?" I asked.

"He's probably in mortal babe heaven," Alexander said. "I appreciate all you've done for him."

"Me? It was nothing."

One other partygoer was not accounted for. Luna was

missing. That could mean only one thing. Trouble.

It was late. Bottles and trash littered the backyard of the Mansion. Alexander and I forced our way through the reveling students. A large crowd had gathered around the gazebo. I pushed through to find Luna, several soccer snobs, and Sebastian sitting in a circle.

In the center, resting on its side, was the empty Transylvania 1972.

The students, unbeknownst to them, were playing a deadly game of spin the bottle.

"We have to stop them," I said.

"The game seems quite uneven. She must be up to something," Alexander said.

The crowd was hooping and hollering, and several guys had formed a line vying for a seat in the circle.

"We're waiting our turn," a guy said to me.

Luna spun the bottle, and it landed on a soccer snob.

"On the cheek, please," she said.

"Are you kidding? Forget it." He got up and walked away.

She spun again. It landed on another soccer snob. "On the cheek, please."

He gently gave her a slobbering kiss on the cheek, to the crowd's delight. She made a face and wiped it off with her sleeve.

Luna twirled the bottle again. It landed on Sebastian.

"On the cheek, I know," he said.

Luna made a deadly stare at Alexander, then gazed at Sebastian. "On the neck, please," she said coyly.

Sebastian was stunned, and the crowd cheered.

She stood up and flipped back one of her pink Wednesday Addams braids to expose her porcelain flesh.

Luna put her waify arms around Sebastian's waist.

"We have to stop this," I said to Alexander. "He's going to bite her!"

"He better not!" Alexander charged forward, but the cheering crowd grew larger, blocking our path to the gazebo.

Sebastian grinned and began to lean in to Luna.

I squeezed myself in between a pair of petite cheerleaders.

Sebastian smiled, revealing two shiny fangs. Luna's eyes closed and she leaned back with delight.

"No!" I screamed.

I jumped between Sebastian and Luna, but at the last moment someone pulled me back.

It was Jagger.

"What are you doing?" voices from the crowd yelled at me.

Alexander and I were mortified. Sebastian was smiling, and Luna was holding her neck, grinning.

She removed her hand. Tiny drops of blood trickled down her neck.

Sebastian turned to me and Alexander, his eyes hazy and his fangs red. He wiped his hand over his mouth and pulled Alexander close.

"I think I'm in love," he declared. "And this time it's for real."